FATALE

ED BRUBAKER SEAN PHILLIPS

FATALE

BOOK ONE
DEATH CHASES ME

By ED BRUBAKER and SEAN PHILLIPS

Colors by Dave Stewart

For Joe Hill and Megan Abbott, who unknowingly gave me these ideas.

IMAGE COMICS, INC.
Robert Kirkman - chief operating officer
Erik Larsen - chief financial officer
Todd McFarlane - president
Marc Silvestri - chief executive officer
Jim Valentino - vice-president

Eric Stephenson - publisher
Todd Martinez - sales & licensing coordinator
Jennifer de Guzman - pr & marketing director
Branwyn Bigglestone - accounts manager
Emily Miller - administrative assistant
Jamie Parreno - marketing assistant
Sarah deLaine - events coordinator
Kevin Yuen - digital rights coordinator
Tyler Shainline - production manager
Drew Gill - art director
Jonathan Chan - design director
Monica Garcia - production artist
Vincent Kukua - production artist
Jana Cook - production artist
www.imagecomics.com

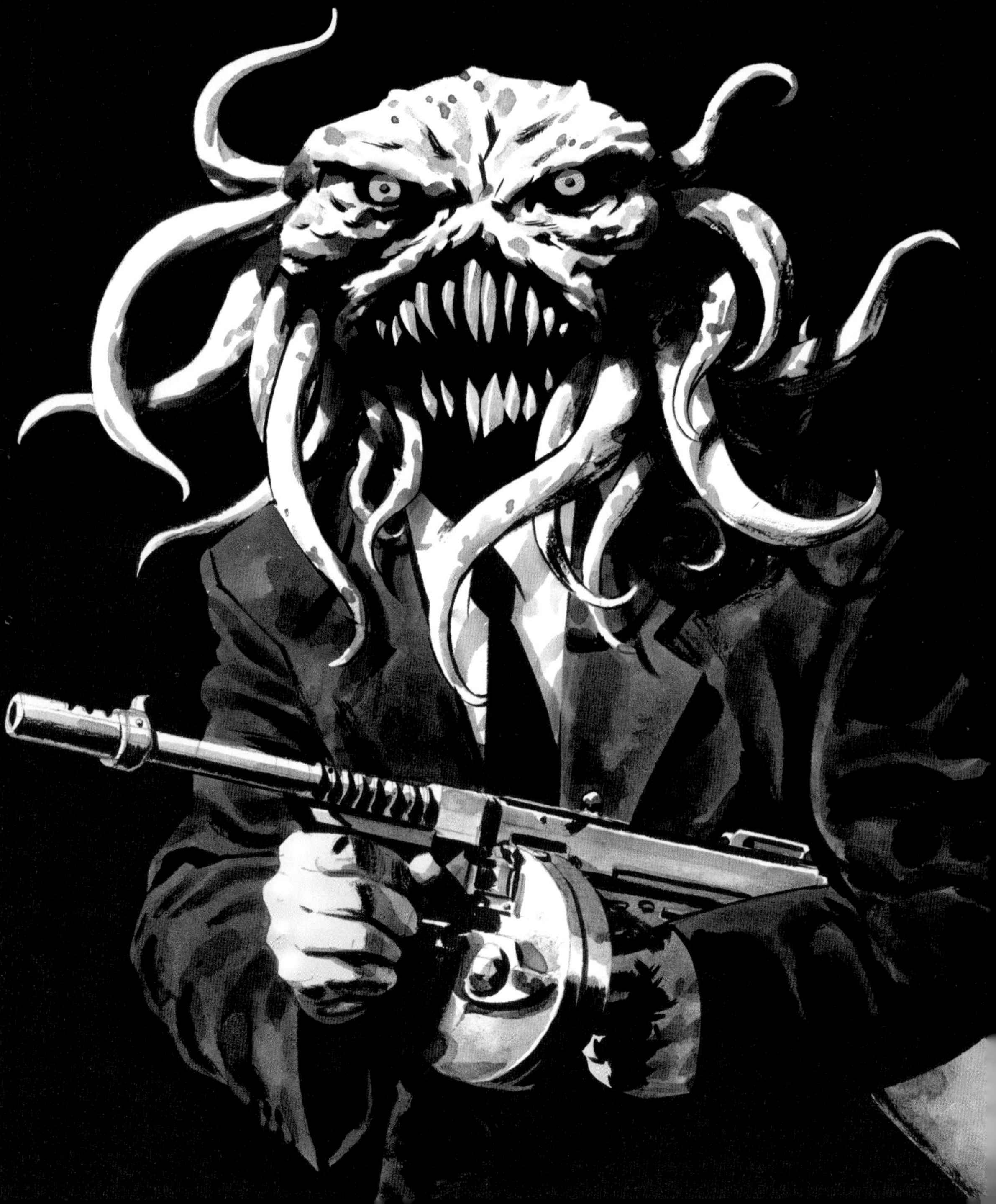

So here's how my entire life went off the tracks in one day.

It started at *Dominic Raines'* funeral...

Prologue

...and of course the weather was as bad as most of the old man's *novels*.

Not that many people would have shown up anyway.

I think my Father was his only *real* friend...

...and Dad'd been in an *institution* for over a decade.

Which is how I ended up executor of the *Raines estate*.

EXCUSE ME... MR *LASH*?

DID YOU WANT THE *PRIEST* TO READ ANYTHING?

NO, MR RAINES WAS AN *ATHEIST*...

I *SEE*... THEN WE'LL LEAVE YOU TO IT.

I didn't see her among the small crowd, which, looking back, is odd.

But I was distracted by the *engravings* on the headstone.

Raines wasn't *just* an atheist... he hated *all* religions.

So what the hell was *this* about?

IT'S A *MADE-UP* SYMBOL...

DOMINIC H. RAINES
1932 - 2011
From Whence He Came

...IF THAT'S WHAT YOU'RE WONDERING.

EXCUSE ME?

MY GRANDMOTHER HAD THEM ON *HER* GRAVE, TOO...

SHE AND MR RAINES WERE *IN LOVE* ONCE.

I THINK THAT SYMBOL WAS SOMETHING *PRIVATE* BETWEEN THEM...

SOME PIECE OF THE *PAST* THEY COULDN'T LET GO OF.

THAT'S... *SAD.*

YEAH... I GUESS IT IS...

I'M NICOLAS LASH... DOMINIC WAS MY *GODFATHER*.

DO PEOPLE CALL YOU "NICK?"

NOT IF I CAN HELP IT.

NICOLAS, THEN. I'M JO.

NICE TO MEET YOU.

IT WAS A NICE CEREMONY... HE WOULD'VE LIKED IT, I THINK.

Later, I'd wonder why my feet felt glued to the ground as she walked away.

How with just a few words, she'd made me feel like some high school kid again.

Dumbstruck.

I didn't know that could still happen.

That night, at Dominic's old place, up north near the coast...

...I thought about what she'd said, about Raines and her grandmother.

Was the bitter old bastard just heartbroken all these years?

Was her grandmother the *muse* he churned out his awful detective novels for?

Bestsellers, *sure*, but garbage.

And then I found what I *knew* would be buried somewhere here...

...an *unpublished* manuscript.

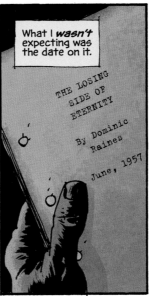

What I *wasn't* expecting was the date on it.

THE LOSING
SIDE OF
ETERNITY

By Dominic
Raines

June, 1957

Raines didn't publish anything until 1960.

Was this his *first novel*?

Suddenly my *inheritance* didn't seem so small, after all.

And just as suddenly...

WHO THE HELL IS *THIS*...?

...All thoughts of good fortune evaporated.

And I realized *exactly* how far out in the woods I actually was.

And how far away the *police* would be.

I had exactly *one* thought then — *RUN THE FUCK AWAY.*

HEY --

STAY OUT OF THE WAY.

GRAAAAHHHH--!

LET'S GO!

It's not until after we run through the woods to her car...

...And we're speeding south on *Highway 1*...

...That I can even bring myself to talk.

WHAT — WHAT WERE YOU... WHY -- ?

I WOULD'VE KNOCKED ON THE FRONT DOOR, BUT I SAW *THEM* HEADING THAT WAY...

I WANTED TO LOOK AT SOME OF DOMINIC'S THINGS...

FOR SOMETHING OF MY *GRAND-MOTHER'S*...

JESUS... WHO *ARE* YOU?

AND WHO THE FUCK *WERE* THOSE GUYS?

I'M SORRY... I SHOULD'VE GOTTEN THERE SOONER.

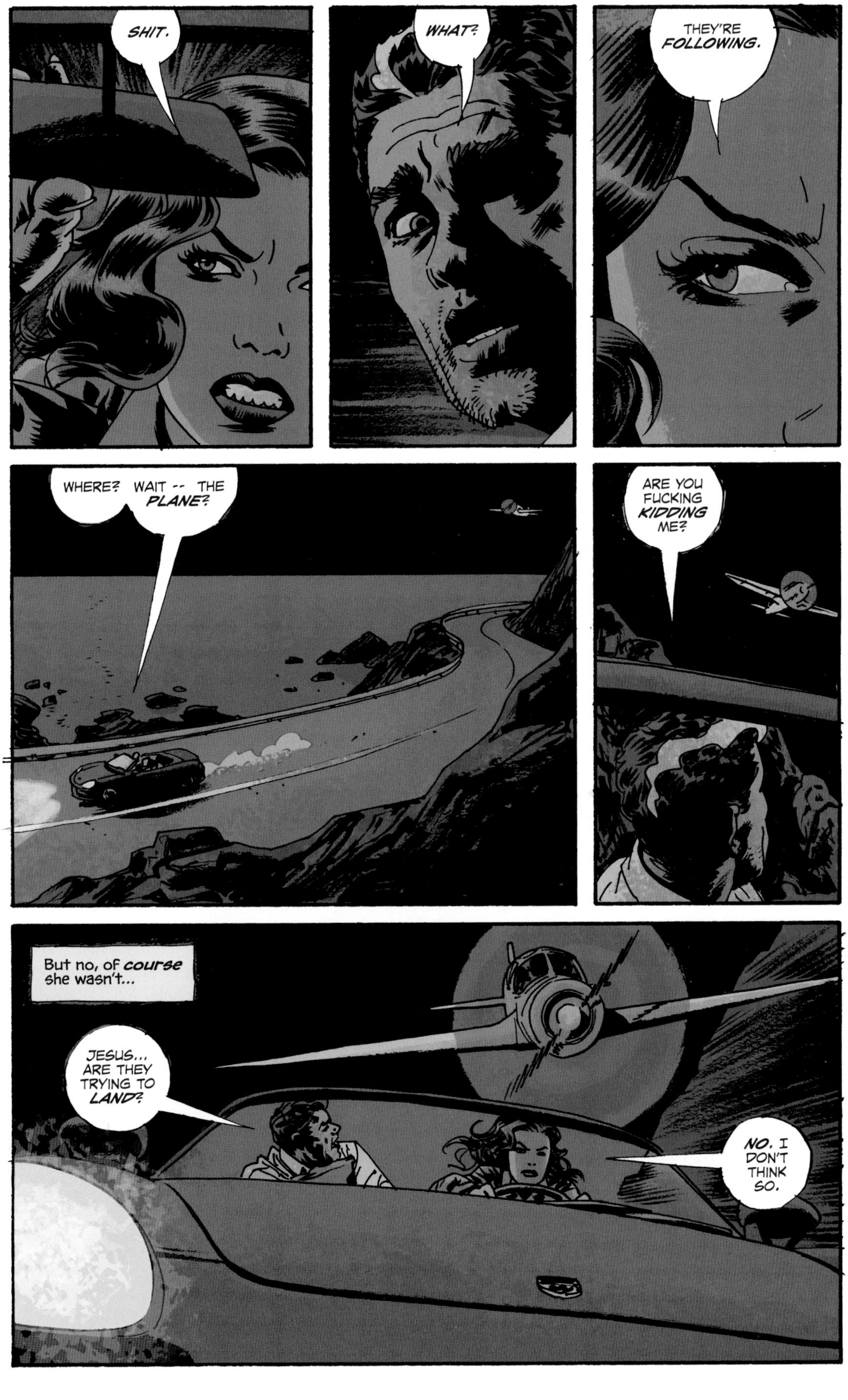
SHIT.
WHAT?
THEY'RE FOLLOWING.
WHERE? WAIT -- THE PLANE?
ARE YOU FUCKING KIDDING ME?
But no, of course she wasn't...
JESUS... ARE THEY TRYING TO LAND?
NO. I DON'T THINK SO.

Because like I said at the beginning...

I'M SORRY, NICOLAS!

This was the day my life went crazy...

JESUS!

The day I met her...

And nothing was ever the same after that.

It couldn't be.

When I wake up, it's five days later, and I'm in a hospital in San Francisco.

I have a vague memory of Jo pulling me to safety...

...And putting Dominic's *manuscript* back into my hands.

The doctors explain how I'm lucky to even be alive.

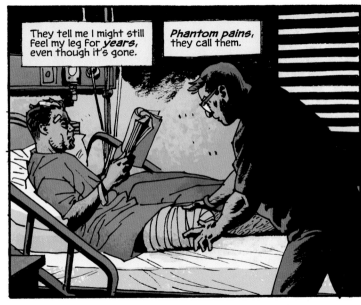

They tell me I might still feel my leg for *years*, even though it's gone.

Phantom pains, they call them.

But the ghost of *my* leg just itches, it doesn't hurt.

The pain will come later, though.

I'm sure of that.

Chapter One

San Francisco – 1956

JOSEPHINE TRIED NOT TO TRADE GLANCES WITH ANYONE IN THE BAR.

SHE DIDN'T KNOW HOW IT WORKED, BUT *EYE CONTACT* SEEMED TO BE PART OF IT.

THANKS.

THE *REPORTER* WAS LATE, WHICH GAVE HER SOME HOPE.

MAYBE HE WOULDN'T SHOW AT ALL.

MAYBE HE'D REALIZED HOW MUCH TROUBLE HE WAS LETTING HIMSELF IN FOR AND HOPPED A TRAIN.

BUT OF COURSE, IN HER EXPERIENCE, TROUBLE WAS *NEVER* THE DETERRENT YOU'D THINK IT SHOULD BE...

SORRY, I GOT A FLAT OUT IN THE *SUNSET*... TOOK FOREVER TO CHANGE.

WHAT'RE YOU DRINKING?

SCOTCH... BUT I'M HERE UNDER *DURESS*...

...SO LET'S NOT PRETEND THIS IS SOME SORT OF *DATE*.

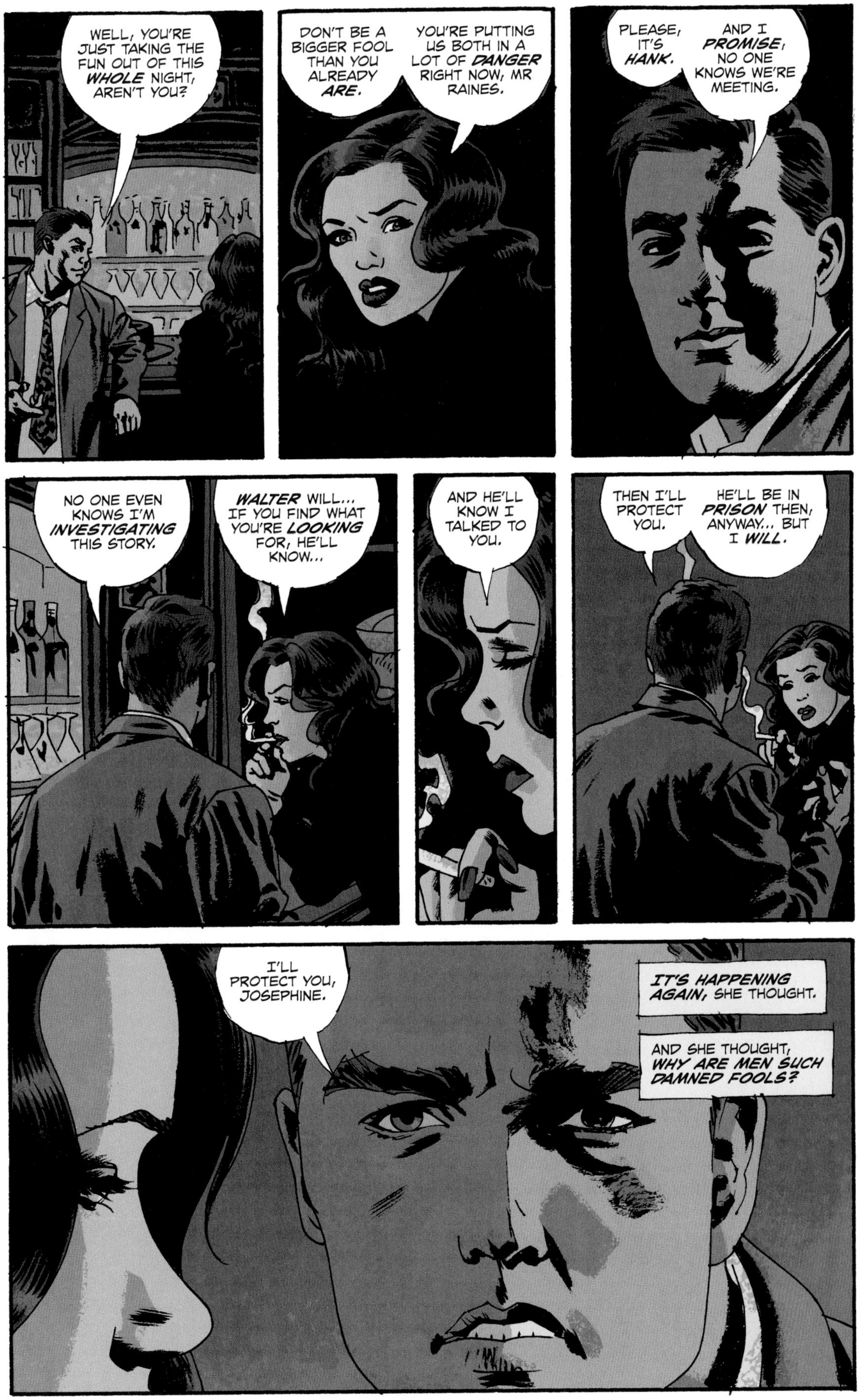
WELL, YOU'RE JUST TAKING THE FUN OUT OF THIS WHOLE NIGHT, AREN'T YOU?
DON'T BE A BIGGER FOOL THAN YOU ALREADY ARE.
YOU'RE PUTTING US BOTH IN A LOT OF DANGER RIGHT NOW, MR RAINES.
PLEASE, IT'S HANK.
AND I PROMISE, NO ONE KNOWS WE'RE MEETING.
NO ONE EVEN KNOWS I'M INVESTIGATING THIS STORY.
WALTER WILL... IF YOU FIND WHAT YOU'RE LOOKING FOR, HE'LL KNOW...
AND HE'LL KNOW I TALKED TO YOU.
THEN I'LL PROTECT YOU.
HE'LL BE IN PRISON THEN, ANYWAY... BUT I WILL.
I'LL PROTECT YOU, JOSEPHINE.
IT'S HAPPENING AGAIN, SHE THOUGHT.
AND SHE THOUGHT, WHY ARE MEN SUCH DAMNED FOOLS?

BUT SHE **NEEDED** THIS HANK RAINES, AND SHE LIKED HIS STUPID FEARLESSNESS...

BECAUSE SHE KNEW HE'D BEEN THAT WAY LONG BEFORE SHE'D MET HIM.

OKAY THEN... HOW MUCH DO YOU KNOW ALREADY?

I KNOW WALT BOOKER AND HIS PARTNER ARE **CROOKED** AS HELL...

...EVEN FOR SAN FRANCISCO COPS.

AND I KNOW **ONE OF THEM** KILLED THAT WITNESS.

BUT I CAN'T PROVE ANYTHING YET.

AND YOU WANT **ME** TO TELL YOU WHERE TO FIND YOUR PROOF, IS THAT IT?

I **DID**, YEAH... BUT NOW I WANT TO KNOW SOMETHING ELSE INSTEAD...

WHAT'S THAT?

HOW A WOMAN LIKE YOU CAN BE **KEPT** BY A MAN LIKE BOOKER...

WHAT THE HELL DOES HE **HAVE** ON YOU?

JESUS, WALT... I *KNOW* IT'S A BAD ONE...

...BUT IF THOSE *UNIFORMS* SEE YOU PUKING YOUR GUTS OUT...

...YOU'LL NEVER HEAR THE *END* OF IT BACK AT THE PRECINCT.

kaff kaaff

FUCK YOUR *MOTHER*, LANNIE...

...I JUST GOT A HANGOVER.

WELL, I HOPE YOU GOT IT ALL UP, THEN...

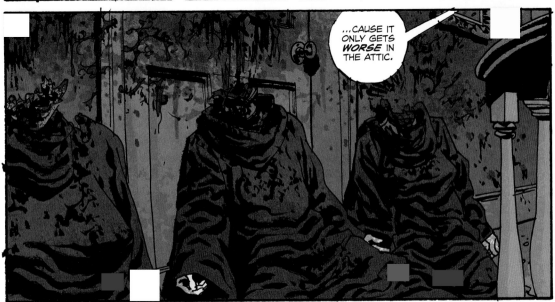

...CAUSE IT ONLY GETS *WORSE* IN THE ATTIC.

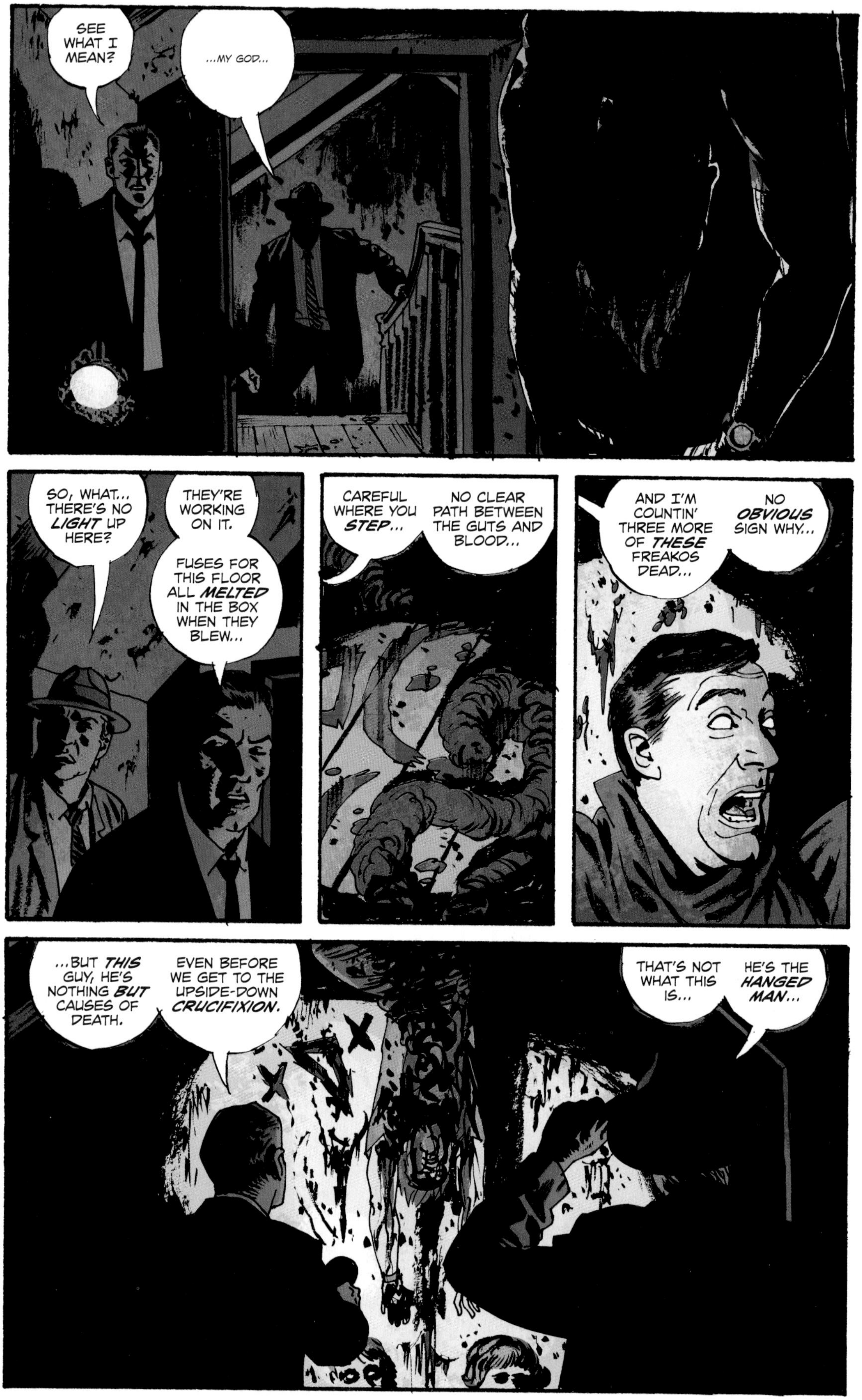
SEE WHAT I MEAN?
...MY GOD...
SO, WHAT... THERE'S NO LIGHT UP HERE?
THEY'RE WORKING ON IT.
FUSES FOR THIS FLOOR ALL MELTED IN THE BOX WHEN THEY BLEW...
CAREFUL WHERE YOU STEP...
NO CLEAR PATH BETWEEN THE GUTS AND BLOOD...
AND I'M COUNTIN' THREE MORE OF THESE FREAKOS DEAD...
NO OBVIOUS SIGN WHY...
...BUT THIS GUY, HE'S NOTHING BUT CAUSES OF DEATH.
EVEN BEFORE WE GET TO THE UPSIDE-DOWN CRUCIFIXION.
THAT'S NOT WHAT THIS IS...
HE'S THE HANGED MAN...

THE HANGMAN?

HANGED... PAST TENSE.

HE'S FROM ALL THAT *OCCULT* CRAP...

...LIKE *THESE* NITWITS.

FIND ANYTHING?

NAH... NO WALLETS, EVEN.

PROBABLY DOWNSTAIRS.

LOOKED LIKE THE WHOLE *CULT* WAS LIVIN' DOWN THERE...

...UH HUNH...

YOU EVER SEEN *ANYTHING* LIKE THIS, WALT?

YEAH. BUT JUST ONCE...

OVER IN EUROPE... IN THE *WAR.*

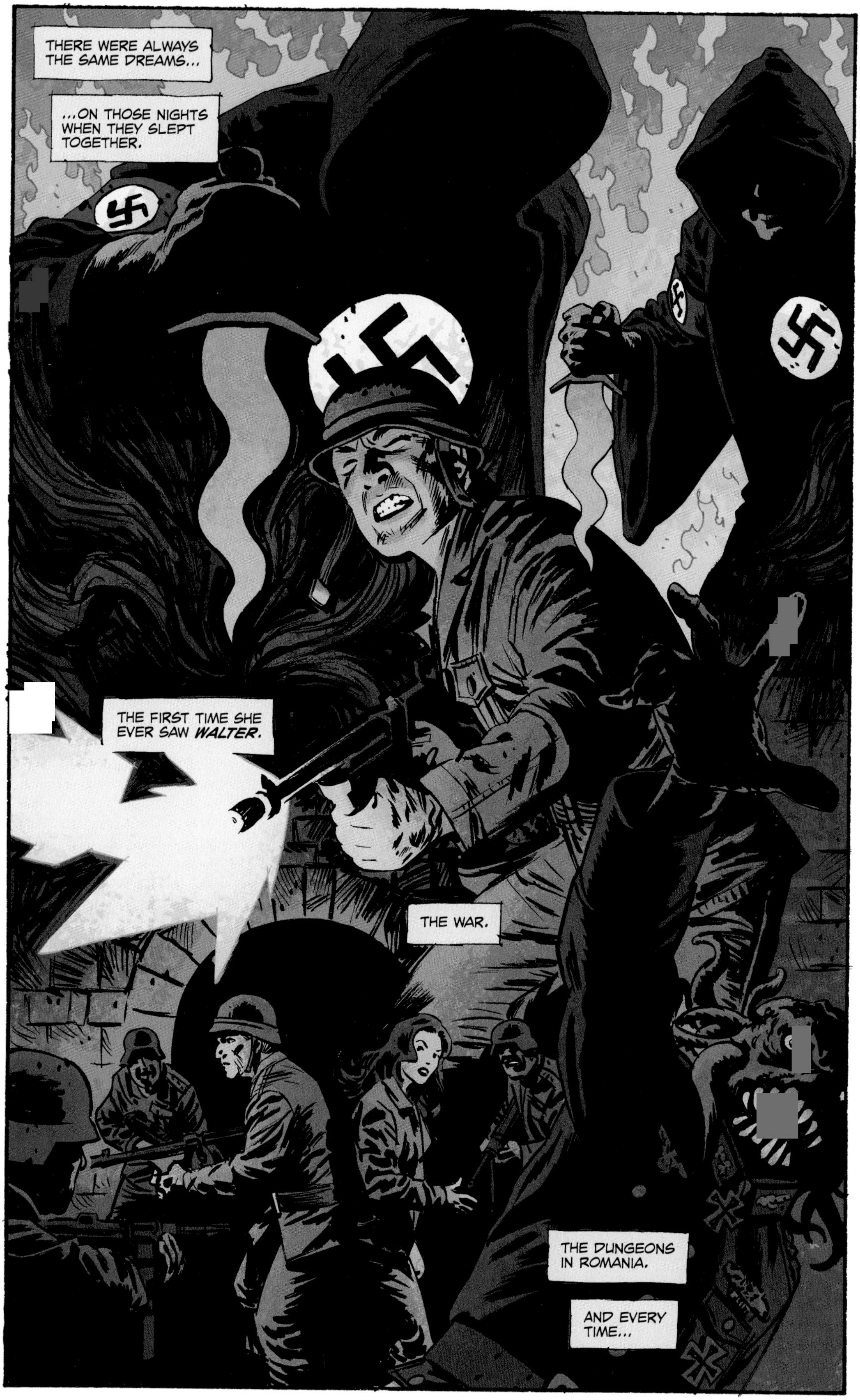
THERE WERE ALWAYS THE SAME DREAMS...
...ON THOSE NIGHTS WHEN THEY SLEPT TOGETHER.
THE FIRST TIME SHE EVER SAW *WALTER*.
THE WAR.
THE DUNGEONS IN ROMANIA.
AND EVERY TIME...

...SHE STILL WOKE UP SHIVERING.

HUUUH –

LIKE SHE'D STEPPED *RIGHT* OUT OF THAT MOMENT IN TIME.

WALTER WAS DOWN THE HALLWAY IN THE WATER CLOSET, *VOMITING* AGAIN.

HE'D BECOME SO FRAGILE LATELY.

WHEN HE EVEN SHOWED UP AT ALL.

WHICH WAS LESS AND LESS THE PAST FEW YEARS.

JUST ENOUGH TO MAKE SURE SHE WAS STILL *HIS*.

BUT THE WAY HE LOOKED AT HER HAD GOTTEN ALL *TWISTED-UP* SOMEHOW.

AND JOSEPHINE DIDN'T *RECOGNIZE* WHAT SHE SAW IN HIS EYES ANYMORE.

SHE JUST KNEW SHE WAS RUNNING OUT OF TIME.

SHE WAITED UNTIL SHE HEARD WALTER'S CAR DRIVE AWAY...

AND THEN SHE STARTED THINKING ABOUT THE REPORTER.

THINKING AS HARD AS SHE COULD.

...JESUS...

HANK WAS IN DEEP ALREADY... AND HE KNEW IT.

HE WISHED HE'D NEVER MET JOSEPHINE.

WISHED HE'D NEVER FOLLOWED BOOKER BACK TO HER APARTMENT.

NOW IT WAS LIKE HE WAS INFECTED... EVERY TIME HE CLOSED HIS EYES...

IT JUST WASN'T FAIR...

THIS WASN'T THE KIND OF SECRET HE'D BEEN TRYING TO UNCOVER.

HE SHOULD BE THINKING ABOUT HIS WIFE; HIS CHILD ON THE WAY...

HE SHOULD BE THINKING ABOUT THEIR FUTURE PLANS...

NOT OBSESSING ABOUT CORRUPT COPS...

...AND THE WOMEN THEY SLEEP WITH.

BUT HE CAN'T CONTROL HIS MIND AND HE'S NEVER FELT *ANYTHING* LIKE THIS BEFORE.

JUST THINKING HER NAME WAS LIKE A PUNCH IN HIS GUTS.

AND NOW HE COULDN'T EVEN SLEEP.

ALL HE COULD DO WAS TRY TO FIGURE OUT HOW HE WAS GOING TO SAVE HER FROM THAT BASTARD *BOOKER*.

THE CARD WALT BOOKER HAD TAKEN OFF THE CULTIST WAS FOR AN *OPIUM DEN* IN CHINATOWN.

NOT A PART OF THE CITY WHERE HE WANTED TO START TROUBLE.

HE HOPED THE MEN HE WAS *LOOKING FOR* WOULD FEEL THE SAME.

UNNN...

WHY COULDN'T JO'S MAGIC WORK FOR HIM TOO?

WHY DID SHE GET TO STAY THE SAME...

...WHILE HE WAS COUGHING UP CHUNKS OF HIS LUNGS?

HE ALREADY FELT OLD AND WITHERED NEXT TO HER...

...CANCER WAS JUST ADDING INJURY TO INSULT.

ON HIS WORST DAYS, HE DIDN'T EVEN WANT TO THINK ABOUT HER.

AND HE HAD NEVER IMAGINED THAT DAY WOULD COME.

BUT WHAT GOOD WAS IT LOVING SOMEONE *SO PERFECT*...

...WHEN YOU WERE WATCHING YOURSELF CRUMBLE TO *DUST* EVERY MORNING IN THE MIRROR?

BIG MISTAKE. YOU'VE GONE FAR OFF YOUR MAP, POLICEMAN...

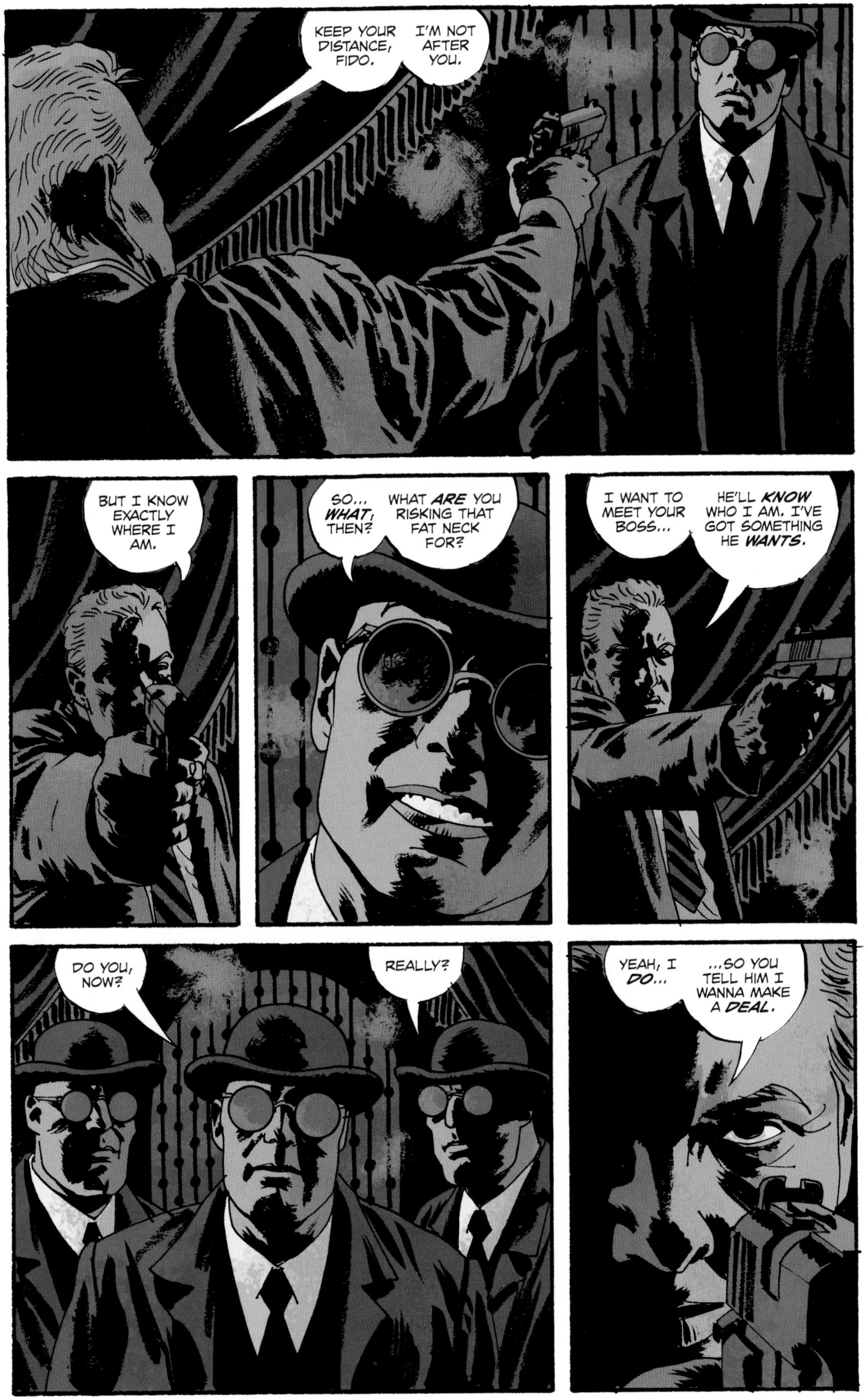
KEEP YOUR DISTANCE, FIDO.
I'M NOT AFTER YOU.
BUT I KNOW EXACTLY WHERE I AM.
SO... WHAT, THEN?
WHAT ARE YOU RISKING THAT FAT NECK FOR?
I WANT TO MEET YOUR BOSS...
HE'LL KNOW WHO I AM. I'VE GOT SOMETHING HE WANTS.
DO YOU, NOW?
REALLY?
YEAH, I DO...
...SO YOU TELL HIM I WANNA MAKE A DEAL.

Chapter
Two

JOSEPHINE KNEW THE LANDLORD WOULD BE NO PROBLEM.

SHE BARELY EVEN HAD TO PUSH.

SURE, YEAH... I GOT A LIGHT...

THANKS, LOUIE.

NOW THEN... YOU SAID SOMETHING ABOUT A *KEY?*

OH, UH... YEAH, YEAH...

JUST USE MY *PASSKEY.*

AND YOU'RE SURE MR BOOKER SAID IT'S OKAY?

OH, I'M *SURE...*

IT'D TAKE *MORE* EFFORT TO BE SURE HE KEPT HER *VISIT* TO HIMSELF.

SHE'D FEEL THE COLD TENDRILS OF THE UNIVERSE TOUCH WHAT WAS LEFT OF HER HEART THEN.

BUT SHE HADN'T SEEN OR HEARD FROM WALTER IN OVER A WEEK NOW...

AND IT FELT STRANGE SAYING IT, BUT TIME *WASN'T* ON HER SIDE.

NOT NOW.

OKAY, WALTER...

GIVE ME A HINT...

SEEING PICTURES OF HIM FROM WHEN HE WAS YOUNG MAKES HER FEEL ILL.

SHE TRUSTED WALTER TO KEEP HER SECRETS -- TO KEEP HER SAFE -- FOR SO LONG.

SHE TAUGHT HIM EVERYTHING THE OLD WOMAN HAD SHOWN HER.

SHE'D EVEN *LOVED* HIM, AS MUCH AS THAT WAS POSSIBLE.

SHE HATES HERSELF... FOR WANTING TO SURVIVE THIS BADLY.

FOR THE THINGS SHE'S DONE, AND THE THINGS SHE'S WILLING TO DO.

SHE CAN STILL FEEL HANK'S HANDS ON HER.

STILL TASTE HIM ON HER LIPS.

AND SHE HATES HERSELF FOR THAT, TOO.

SHE THINKS ABOUT HIS WIFE... PICTURES HER *WAITING UP*...

...LYING TO HERSELF THAT HER HUSBAND IS WORKING LATE.

OR *OUT ALL NIGHT* CHASING A LEAD.

AND SHE WANTS TO CRY; FOR WHAT SHE'S DOING TO THIS WOMAN.

BUT SHE *DOESN'T*...

...BECAUSE IT'S NOT *JUST* ABOUT SURVIVAL.

DAMN YOU, WALTER...

YOU *HAD* TO BE KEEPING IT IN THERE...

WHERE *IS* IT?

THERE ARE PEOPLE WITH *FAR WORSE* THINGS THAN DEATH IN MIND FOR HER.

HEY... IS THIS TONIGHT'S FINAL?

YEP. YOU AN' YER PAL *RAINES* MADE THE *FRONT PAGE.*

NO... THAT CAN'T BE RIGHT...

HEY, *CAREFUL,* JOHNNY... I STILL GOTTA GET THAT DOWN TO THE PRESSES.

NICE GOIN' ON THE *PIC,* THOUGH.

THAT'S *"MAYDAY"* LUCCARELLI, RIGHT?

YEAH... BUT, THIS WASN'T SUPPOSED TO RUN *YET.*

WE WERE BUILDING A *BIGGER* STORY HERE.

WHAT THE HELL IS HANK *DOING?*

FUCK IF I KNOW... BUT MACAVITY SAYS YOU'RE SELLIN' A LOTTA *PAPERS* TONIGHT, KID.

YOU TWO ARE FRIGGIN' *HEROES...*

COURSE... I'M GUESSIN' THOSE *COPS* MIGHT NOT SEE IT THAT WAY.

KNN CH

ALL RIGHT, YA *FREAKO* SONS OF BITCHES...

...EVERYBODY JUST *STAY PUT!*

DON'T MAKE THIS GET UGLY!

JESUS, LANNIE... EASE UP.

LOOK AT 'EM...

THESE SAD SACKS OF SHIT AREN'T GONNA –

KRAAK

WALT!

MOTHERFUCKER...

HEY --
SHITBIRD!

NO. THAT
ONE'S
MINE.

BUT THE LITTLE DEATH-
WORSHIPPING JUNKIE WAS
FASTER THAN HE LOOKED.

BASTARD.

WALT FELT LIKE HIS
LUNGS WERE GOING
TO EXPLODE.

AND THAT JUST
MADE HIM ANGRIER.

THEY'D SPENT DAYS ROUNDING-UP SAN FRANCISCO'S CRAZIEST WEIRDOS.

AND THIS WAS A CITY WITH *NO SHORTAGE* OF THAT TYPE.

FREAKS SPEAKING IN TONGUES WHILE CARVING SYMBOLS INTO THE BACKS OF LOST CHILDREN...

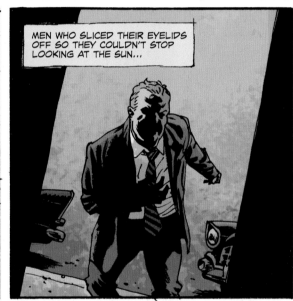

MEN WHO SLICED THEIR EYELIDS OFF SO THEY COULDN'T STOP LOOKING AT THE SUN...

CACKLING FOOLS WHO SAW SOME *GRAND DESIGN* IN THE WORLD'S MISERY...

A WEEK AMONG THE STENCH OF INSANITY...

WAIT... LOOK...

...AND STILL *NO WORD* BACK ON HIS OFFER TO THE *REAL* MONSTER.

KRAAK

UHTT --

THE BASTARD WAS GOING TO JUST LET HIM DIE.

KRAAK

THAT WAS BECOMING CLEAR NOW.

KNNCCH

...WUUH...

AND IT WAS GOING TO BE A PAINFUL DEATH.

HAKK HAKK HAKKK !!

HA-RAKK HAKK HAKKK !!

...Walter Booker...

...the Bishop will meet with you...

...He will hear your prayers...

...Tonight... when you are alone...

...he will find you...

JESUS...

...WHAA...? AHH... AHH...

WALT? YOU OKAY HERE?

YEAH... PRICK GOT IN A LUCKY SHOT, IS ALL...

HELP ME GET 'IM ON HIS FEET.

CHRIST... I THINK YOU FRACTURED THIS BOZO'S *SKULL*, PARTNER.

YEAH... LET'S HOPE.

AND FOR A SECOND, THAT'S JUST WHAT WALTER BOOKER DID: *HOPE.*

BUT ONLY FOR A SECOND.

BECAUSE THERE'D BE NO TURNING BACK NOW.

WHAT THE **HELL**, HANK??!

YOU DON'T GIVE ME **ANY NOTICE** YOU TURNED IN THAT STORY?

AHH, **CRAP**, JOHNNY... I'M SORRY.

JUST GOT CAUGHT UP IN THE RUSH TO PRESS...

HERE, LEMME GET YOUR FIRST ROUND...

THAT'S NOT REALLY THE **POINT**, HANK.

WE SPENT ALL THOSE NIGHTS ON **STAKEOUT**... FOR WHAT?

THOUGHT WE WERE WAITIN' 'TIL WE HAD ENOUGH TO **BRING 'EM DOWN**.

I KNOW, I JUST... I **RETHOUGHT** THINGS.

DECIDED TO STIR UP SOME SHIT, SEE WHAT HAPPENS.

NO, YOU WENT FOR **SCANDAL** OVER PROOF.

YOU WANNA BE **FAMOUS**, HANK, IS THAT IT?

THAT HURTS. YOU KNOW ME **BETTER** THAN THAT.

YEAH, I KNOW YOU **TOO** WELL.

AN' I **TOLD** **YOU** TO STAY AWAY FROM BOOKER'S WOMAN.

BUT YOU JUST **COULDN'T** STOP YOURSELF, COULD YOU?

JOHNNY – KID – IT'S **NOT** LIKE THAT...

I'M A PHOTOGRAPHER, HANK... SO I SEE DETAILS...

...AND I **KNOW** THAT AIN'T SYLVIA'S **LIPSTICK** ON YOUR COLLAR, PAL.

JOHNNY WAS RIGHT, OF COURSE. HANK COULD LIE AND SAY HE'D TRIED TO DO THE RIGHT THING... TRIED TO **RESIST**...

BUT HE HADN'T.

AND HE DIDN'T EVEN FEEL **GUILTY** ABOUT IT. THAT WAS THE STRANGE PART.

NO, EVERY MOMENT HE SPENT WITH JOSEPHINE...

FELT LIKE GIVING IN TO DESTINY.

SOMEHOW, PLOTTING DECEIT AND EVEN POSSIBLY MURDER...

CHEATING ON HIS WIFE...

SHE MADE IT ALL SEEM *ROMANTIC.*

THERE WERE LONG DRIVES IN THE AFTERNOON...

SLOW EVENINGS...

SHE DEFLECTED NEARLY EVERY QUESTION ABOUT HER PAST.

BUT EACH NON-ANSWER MADE HIM FEEL HE KNEW HER BETTER.

SYMPATHY SWELLED IN HIS CHEST UNTIL HE WANTED TO CRY.

HE DOESN'T *HIT* YOU OR ANYTHING LIKE THAT... DOES HE?

NO... WALTER'S ABUSE TAKES *OTHER* FORMS...

OR IT HAS *SO FAR,* AT LEAST...

HE *IS* A VIOLENT MAN, THOUGH.

YOU DON'T HAVE TO TELL *ME*... I'VE SEEN THE EVIDENCE.

HE *WASN'T* ALWAYS LIKE THAT.

HE WAS... *NOBLE,* ONCE.

MUST'VE BEEN A *LONG* TIME AGO...

HE'S *FAR* FROM THAT NOW.

TIME JUST WEARS ON SOME PEOPLE *HARDER* THAN OTHERS, HANK...

WALTER DIDN'T *START OUT* CORRUPT, IS WHAT I'M SAYING...

LIFE JUST DIDN'T GO AS PLANNED.

BUT YOU STILL WANT TO *DO IT,* RIGHT?

YOU STILL WANNA GET *RID* OF HIM?

YES, BUT HOW *WE* DECIDED... JUST MAKE HIS LIFE HELL.

NOTHING THAT'LL PUT HIM BEHIND BARS RIGHT AWAY.

I MUCH PREFER THE PLAN THAT *DOES* PUT HIM BEHIND BARS.

I KNOW *YOU* DO, BUT WALTER'S GOT SOMETHING OF MINE... A SORT OF *HEIRLOOM.*

AND IF I'M GOING TO *REALLY* GET FREE OF HIM...

WELL... LET'S JUST SAY IT'S PRETTY VALUABLE.

AND YOU THINK HE'LL GO RUNNING FOR IT WHEN THE WALLS START CLOSING IN?

I *DO,* YES...

HE'LL BE LOOKING FOR WHATEVER HE'S *GOT* THAT HE CAN TRADE OR SELL.

SO, TAKE A *MAD* DOG AND GIVE HIM *RABIES*... THAT'S YOUR PLAN?

EVEN A RABID DOG CAN HAVE ITS *USES.*

HE SHOULD'VE SAID NO.

RATTLING BOOKER AND DALTON'S CAGES WAS STUPID.

BUT HE WAS FAR PAST DENYING JOSEPHINE ANYTHING.

EVERYTHING SHE DID OR SAID BROKE HIM A LITTLE MORE.

EVEN HER SUPERSTITIONS...

WHAT IS THAT *THING* YOU ALWAYS DRAW?

IT'S STUPID, I KNOW... MY MAMA TAUGHT THAT TO ME...

IT'S SO NO ONE, NOT EVEN *GOD*, CAN *SEE YOU* WHEN YOU SIN.

OH YEAH? DOES IT WORK?

DON'T KNOW.

MAMA WASN'T MUCH OF A SINNER, REALLY...

STILL... BETTER SAFE THAN SORRY.

SO, YOU REALLY *ARE* THIS DESPERATE?

I MEAN, I CAN SMELL YOU FROM HERE... SO I GET IT.

BUT STILL... SHE MUST BE SLIPPING.

I THOUGHT YOU SAID...?

WHAT, *HIM?*

IT WAS *HIS* SACRIFICE THAT BROUGHT US TOGETHER.

BUT DON'T WORRY, HE WAS ONE OF *OURS*... NOT YOURS.

ARE YOU THE CAUSE OF IT?

THE CLOAK AND HOOD BRIGADE *SUICIDES...?* ALL THEIR *FREAKED-OUT* NASTINESS?

I HAVE *NO IDEA* WHAT YOU'RE TALKING ABOUT, SERGEANT BOOKER.

BUT THERE ARE *COSTS* TO DOING BUSINESS...

ANY KIND OF BUSINESS...

UH HUNH...

SO, *CANCER?* THAT'S ALL IT TOOK?

AND TO THINK I WAS *IMPRESSED* WITH YOU ONCE.

I DON'T GIVE *TWO SHITS* ABOUT WHAT YOU *THINK,* MONSTER.

I JUST WANNA KNOW IF YOU CAN DO IT?

HEH HEH...

YOU EVER WONDER WHY YOUR *CRYPTOGRAPHER* FRIEND WENT CRAZY TRANSLATING THAT PAGE...

BUT YOU WERE *FINE?*

HE'S IN THE *LATRINE* WITH A GUN IN HIS MOUTH...

...AND YOU'RE RACING OFF LIKE SOME EXPLORER WITH A *TREASURE MAP*.

NO. I NEVER WONDERED.

YOU CAN DELIVER THE *GIRL*?

YOU WOULDN'T *BE HERE* IF I COULDN'T.

IT WON'T BE PLEASANT... WHAT YOU HAVE TO DO...

BUT WE CAN GET RID OF YOUR CANCER...

THAT'LL GIVE YOU AT LEAST ANOTHER TWENTY YEARS TO REGRET THIS...

BUT YOU'VE GOT OTHER PROBLEMS, TOO...

I TAKE IT YOU DIDN'T PICK UP A *PAPER* TONIGHT?

NO...

NICE SHOT OF YOU AND YOUR PARTNER... AND THAT'S "MAYDAY" LUCCARELLI YOU'RE WITH, RIGHT?

SEE, THAT WAS *STUPID*, WALTER...

SON OF A BITCH.

MEETING WITH THE MOBSTER YOU HELPED GET FREE OF A *MURDER* CHARGE.

TAKING A *PAYOFF* IN BROAD DAYLIGHT.

FUCK.

YEAH, THAT'S GONNA *COMPLICATE* THINGS...

...HAVING YOUR BOSSES RAKING YOU OVER THE COALS.

BUT SINCE WE'RE MAKING A BARGAIN HERE...

...I GUESS I CAN CLEAN UP *THAT* MESS, TOO.

HANK HAD GOTTEN TOO DRUNK.

BUT MISSING HER HURT... IN HIS BODY AND HIS MIND.

SO HE POURED ALCOHOL ON THE WOUNDS.

HE'D WANTED THIS WHEN HE WAS YOUNG... THAT PURE PASSION, THAT DEADLY HEAT...

BUT THE TIMES HE'D COME *CLOSE* WERE ALL ILLUSION.

A FEW WEEKS OF IMAGINING SOME GIRL WAS SOMETHING SHE *WASN'T*...

BEFORE THE SHOUTING AND SLAMMING DOORS BEGAN...

POLICE ON THE TAKE?

NOW HE REALIZED HE'D BEEN *LUCKY* BEFORE.

THE WAY HE FELT ABOUT JOSEPHINE... IT WAS OUT OF BALANCE WITH THE WORLD.

IT WAS UNFAIR TO EVERYTHING AND EVERYONE ELSE.

WHAT...?

HER SYMBOL... WRITTEN IN LIPSTICK ON A NAPKIN...

WHEN HAD SHE SNUCK THIS INTO HIS POCKET?

...CHRIST, JO...

SILLY GIRL, HE THOUGHT.

POWELL AND MARKET

50

BUT ONLY FOR A SECOND.

SYLVIA RAINES HAD KNOWN ALL WEEK SOMETHING WAS *WRONG* WITH HER HUSBAND.

BUT SHE HAD NO IDEA SHE WAS ABOUT TO GET HER *HEART* BROKEN AGAIN.

...OH... MY...

SHE'D ALWAYS THOUGHT HANK WAS *DIFFERENT* THAN OTHER MEN...

...STUPID STUPID... DAMN IT...

SHE'D BELIEVED IN HIM... HIS JOURNALISTIC CRUSADES, HIS RIGHTEOUSNESS...

HOW COULD SHE HAVE BEEN SO WRONG?

AND THEIR *CHILD* IS DUE IN JUST OVER A MONTH.

HOW COULD HE *DO THIS* TO HER?

BNNNG BONG

COMING!

GOOD MORNING, MA'AM... IS THIS THE RESIDENCE OF *DOMINIC RAINES*?

IT *IS*... BUT HE GOES BY HIS MIDDLE NAME, HENRY — WELL, *HANK*.

AND HE LEFT FOR *WORK* AN HOUR AGO.

YES, I KNOW... BUT I WAS HOPING I COULD TALK TO *YOU*, ACTUALLY.

IS THIS ABOUT *MY HUSBAND*?

YES. ABOUT AN *AWARD* HE'S UP FOR.

BUT THAT'S *TOP SECRET*... JUST BETWEEN YOU AN' ME.

WELL, I SUPPOSE YOU'D BETTER COME IN, THEN, MISTER...?

BISHOP... MR BISHOP. AND I PROMISE...

...THIS WON'T TAKE *ANY TIME* AT ALL.

Interlude

Raines's manor house is a *mess* by the time I manage to get back to it.

Like someone searched it quickly... and savagely.

Like it's been brutalized.

But there's no sign of the man Josephine *shot* in the hallway...

...And I don't mention *any* of that craziness to the police.

-- NO IDEA HOW YOU ENDED UP IN THAT CAR BEFORE THE *ACCIDENT?*

NO... LAST THING I REMEMBER IS THE FUNERAL...

THEN -- *THIS...*

They don't like it, but they don't push too much.

IF ANYTHING COMES BACK TO YOU, ANYTHING *AT ALL...* YOU CALL US, OKAY?

PROBABLY JUST SOME ASSHOLE KIDS WHO BROKE IN AND DID ALL THIS...

OR *TWEAKERS.*

YEAH. BUT 'TIL YOU REMEMBER MORE ABOUT THAT NIGHT...

...I WOULDN'T ADVISE *STAYIN'* OUT HERE.

MIGHT NOT BE *SAFE...* NOT IN YOUR CONDITION.

As if I *needed* to be told.

This was the last place I wanted to be.

I only came back at all to try to find something more about *her*.

But my hands shake as I sift through the wreckage.

Every creak this old house makes brings me closer to a panic attack.

And there's nothing left here now... if there ever was.

No hidden photo album. No cigar box of old love letters.

Just me, in a house filling with shadows.

YOU NEED SOME HELP?

NAH, I GOT IT...

So all I had to go on was Dominic's unpublished manuscript...

...Which was a *puzzle* in itself.

I'd read the book ten times in the month since the explosion...

...Expecting to find some kind of answer for what happened to me in its pages.

But if there was one in there, I wasn't seeing it.

The lead character, Roderick Graves, was clearly a stand-in for Dominic...

But the story was... surreal, sort of.

Graves is a reporter on a *lost weekend* after the sudden death of his wife.

Or... he's on the run from the mafia.

Or maybe *both*.

Like I said, it's a bit surreal.

It was also probably the best thing Raines *ever* wrote. So why the hell hadn't he published it?

--SORRY TO HEAR ABOUT YOUR *ACCIDENT*, NICOLAS.

I SAW IT ON THE NEWS... *REALLY* BIZARRE, AND FUCKED UP.

THANKS, MAGGIE...

...BUT I'M GUESSING THAT'S *NOT* WHY YOU CAME ALL THE WAY OUT FROM NEW YORK.

NO. UH.., I, UH.,, HEARD A RUMOR DOMINIC HAD SOME UNFINISHED MATERIAL HIDDEN AWAY UP THERE.,,

AND IF THAT *IS* THE CASE... THE PUBLISHER'S AUTHORIZED ME TO OFFER A *CONSIDERABLE* ADVANCE.

YOU KNOW, ASSUMING THERE *IS* A BOOK...

I'M SORRY.

OKAY, WELL... I'LL LET YOU KNOW IF I *FIND* ANYTHING, MAGGIE.

PLEASE DO... I'M IN TOWN A FEW MORE DAYS.

What the hell is happening to me? I was thinking.

All I knew was the book was my only link to her...

And there *had* to be a reason the old man never let anyone see it.

But the only part that makes me think of Jo *at all* is a scene where an old woman tells a drunken Graves a bizarre fairy tale.

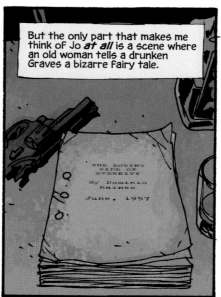

THE LOSING
SIDE OF
ETERNITY

By Dominic
Raines

June, 1957

About a silk ribbon that's wound around the world every night, held in the beak of an owl.

At least I *think* it's an owl, from the description.

And then it finally occurs to me.

Everything in this book is odd. Unreal to some degree.

Except for the death of Graves' wife.

She falls down the stairs while doing the laundry. So *ordinary*.

Which makes me think, is that the part that's real?

Did Dominic have a *wife* I never knew about?

How many secrets was the old bastard keeping?

Hours of digging in the microfilm room at the downtown library proves me right.

Dominic Henry Raines was married in 1955 to Sylvia Maria Bernley.

Announcing the union of Dominic Raines and Sylvia Bernley

It takes another hour to find out the next part of their story...

...And why I *never* heard about this woman.

I only make it halfway through the description of the crime...

...JESUS CHRIST...

...before the ghost of my leg is dragging what's left of me away, as fast as I can go.

Chapter Three

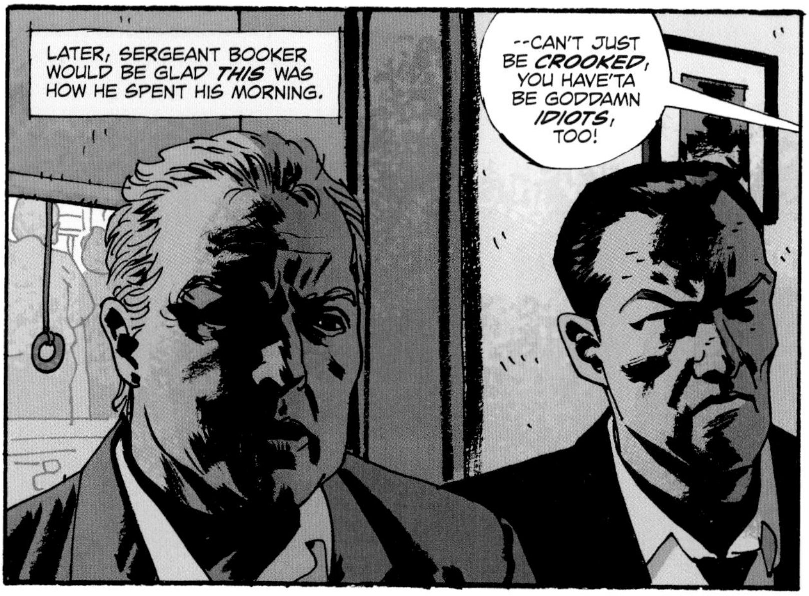
LATER, SERGEANT BOOKER WOULD BE GLAD THIS WAS HOW HE SPENT HIS MORNING.
--CAN'T JUST BE CROOKED, YOU HAVE'TA BE GODDAMN IDIOTS, TOO!

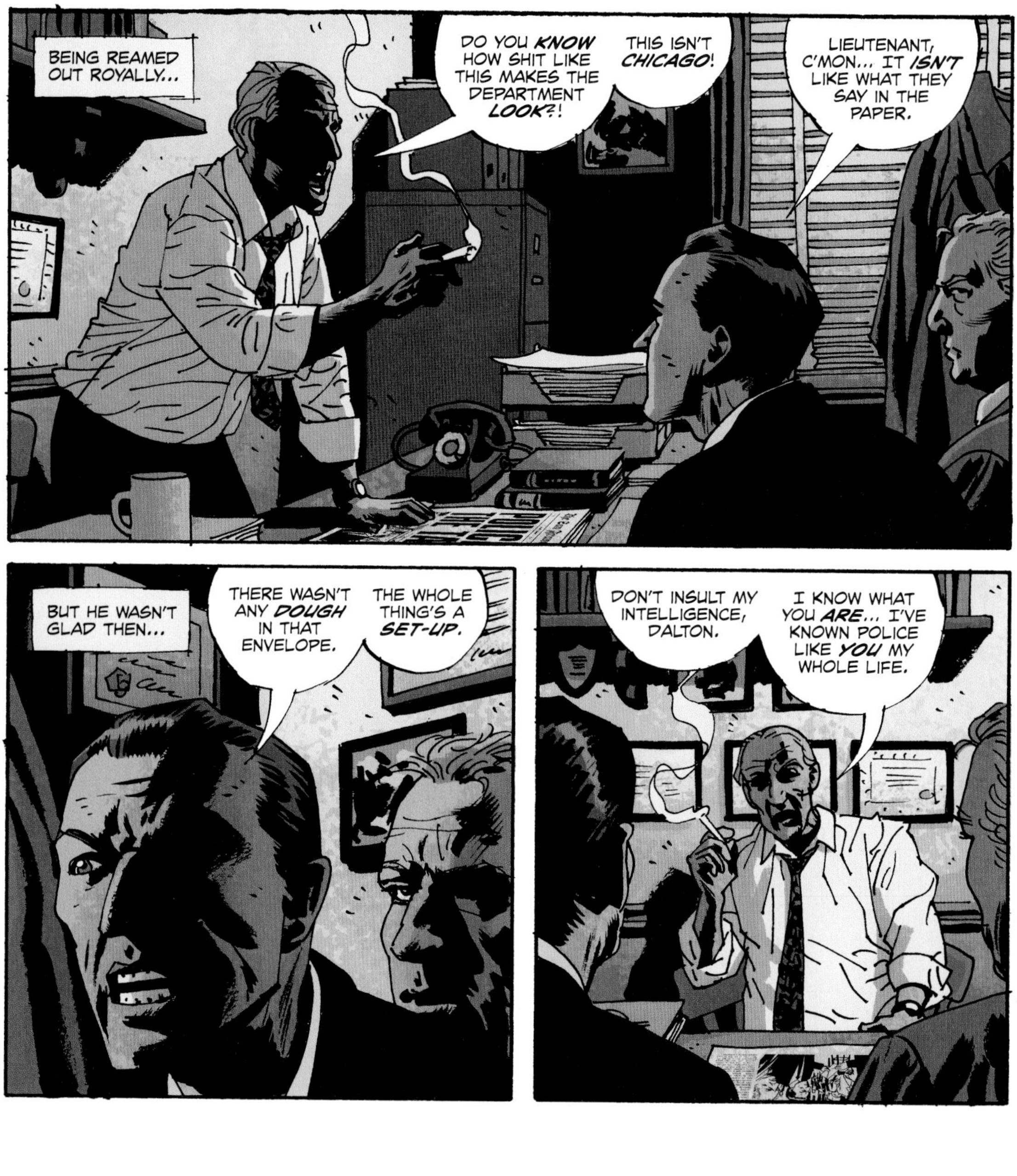
BEING REAMED OUT ROYALLY...
DO YOU KNOW HOW SHIT LIKE THIS MAKES THE DEPARTMENT LOOK?!
THIS ISN'T CHICAGO!
LIEUTENANT, C'MON... IT ISN'T LIKE WHAT THEY SAY IN THE PAPER.
BUT HE WASN'T GLAD THEN...
THERE WASN'T ANY DOUGH IN THAT ENVELOPE.
THE WHOLE THING'S A SET-UP.
DON'T INSULT MY INTELLIGENCE, DALTON.
I KNOW WHAT YOU ARE... I'VE KNOWN POLICE LIKE YOU MY WHOLE LIFE.

WALT DIDN'T LIKE THIS KNOW-NOTHING *DESK HUMPER* ONE BIT.

IF I HAD *MORE* TO GO ON THAN THIS PICTURE, YOU'D BOTH BE WALKING A BEAT...

OR *MAYBE* WALKING AROUND A PRISON YARD.

DIDN'T LIKE HIS LONGWINDED PIOUS BULLSHIT.

BUT THIS REPORTER *WILL* BE QUESTIONED, AS WILL MR LUCCARELLI...

I'M ORDERING A COMPLETE REVIEW.

WHAT'S YOUR *CASELOAD?* WHAT'RE YOU WORKING?

THE CULT THING.

AH... *FINE* THEN. THAT'S A *KIND* OF PUNISHMENT IN ITSELF.

THAT'LL BE YOUR *ONLY* CASE UNTIL MY INVESTIGATION IS OVER.

BUT LATER HE'D REALIZE THEY'D SAT THERE FOR *TWO HOURS* THAT MORNING...

NOW GET THE HELL OUT OF MY SIGHT.

AND HE'D BE GLAD... EVEN *RELIEVED*...

...CAN YOU *DESCRIBE* THE SMELL, SIR?

AND DO YOU SEE ANY *BLOODSTAINS* NEAR THE DOOR?

OR BROKEN GLASS? ANYTHING SUSPICIOUS AT ALL?

...BECAUSE THAT MEANT HE HAD AN *ALIBI*.

JESUS, WE ARE SO SCREWED, PARTNER.

NO. IT'S JUST CHICKEN-SHIT... *INNUENDO.*

STILL, WE GOT SLOPPY. IT'S OUR *OWN* FAULT.

FUCK THAT. NO ONE KNEW WE WERE MEETIN' UP WITH MAYDAY.

DID THEY?

I DIDN'T TELL ANYONE.

WHICH IS A LIE, WALT THINKS.

SHIT. YOU THINK *LUCCARELLI* SET US UP?

I DON'T *KNOW,* LANNIE... MAYBE...

HE'D TOLD JO. HE TOLD HER A LOT OF THINGS HE SHOULDN'T.

HE COULDN'T *HELP* HIMSELF... AND IT KEPT THEM FROM DISCUSSING THE OBVIOUS.

THAT WHATEVER THEY'D ONCE *BEEN* WAS LONG LOST.

JO...?

YOU LOOK FOR MISS JOSEPHINE?

I *DO*, YES...

SHE *LEAVE*, TWO NIGHTS AGO. MAN COME, TAKE HER THINGS AWAY.

SHE STILL OWE RENT.

YES. I'M SURE SHE DOES.

IT HURTS, REALIZING SHE'S MAKING THE FIRST MOVE.

AND THAT ALMOST MAKES HIM LAUGH.

HE THOUGHT HIS HEART COULDN'T BREAK ANY MORE OVER HER.

BUT SOMEWHERE INSIDE, HE'S JUST AS IN LOVE AS HE ALWAYS HAS BEEN.

AND NOW SHE'S GOING TO SCREW EVERYTHING UP...

ALL HIS DESPERATE PLANS.

HEY --

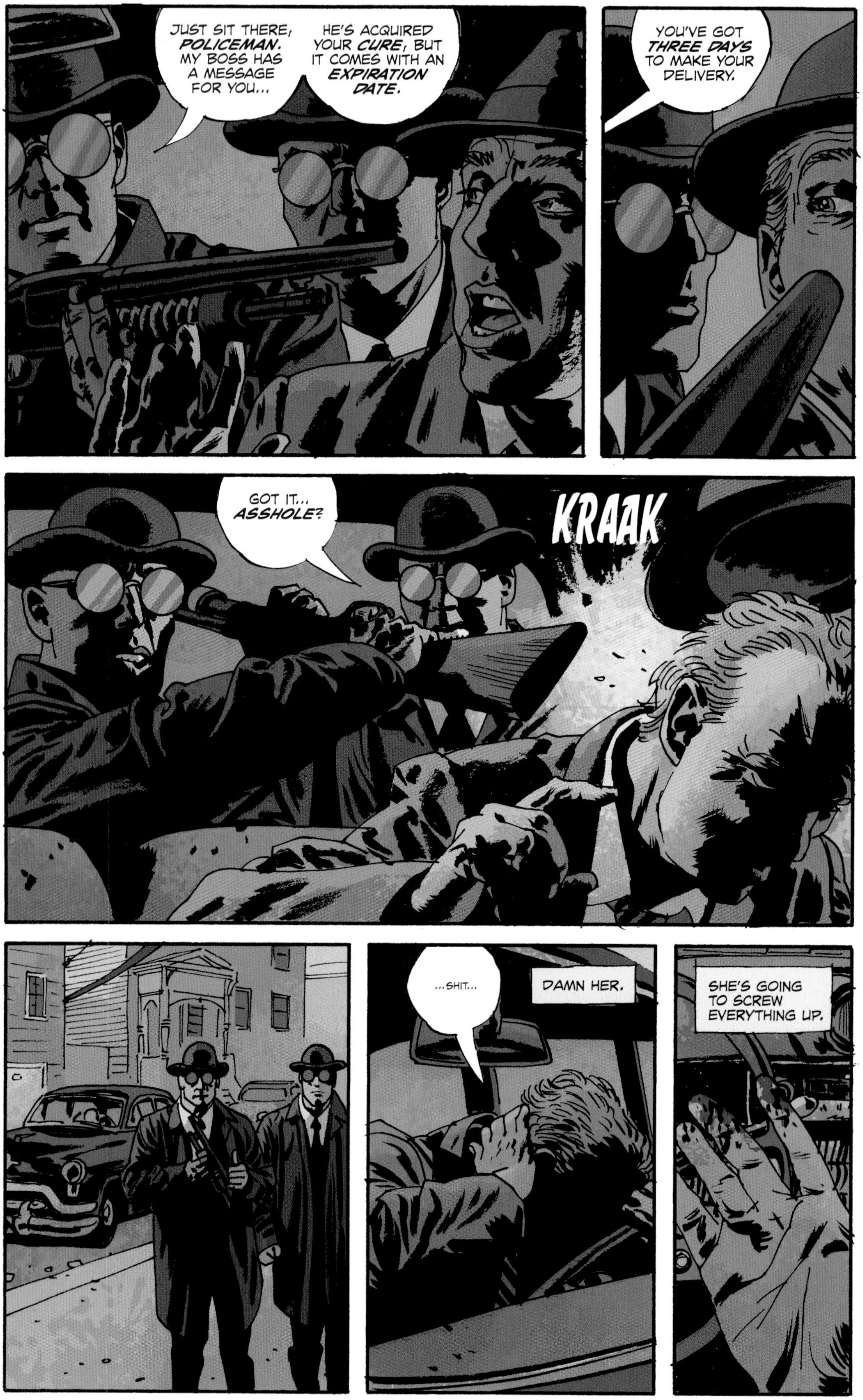
JUST SIT THERE, POLICEMAN. MY BOSS HAS A MESSAGE FOR YOU...
HE'S ACQUIRED YOUR CURE, BUT IT COMES WITH AN EXPIRATION DATE.
YOU'VE GOT THREE DAYS TO MAKE YOUR DELIVERY.
GOT IT... ASSHOLE?
KRAAK
...SHIT...
DAMN HER.
SHE'S GOING TO SCREW EVERYTHING UP.

WHAT ARE YOU DOING?

COME BACK TO BED.

WE SHOULD BE GETTING *BACK*.

HANK HADN'T WANTED TO LEAVE SAN FRANCISCO THAT DAY AT ALL.

NO... LET'S GO OUT.

THERE'S SOMETHING I WANT TO SHOW YOU.

BUT JOSEPHINE HAD *INSISTED*.

SHE'D FELT A CHANGE, LIKE SOMETHING GROWING HEAVY IN THE AIR...

AND SHE'D WOKEN UP UNEASY. ANXIOUS.

IT WAS SAFER FOR HANK TO STAY OUT OF SIGHT, ANYWAY...

EVEN THOUGH THE STUBBORN FOOL DIDN'T REALIZE IT.

BUT THEN, HE STILL HAD NO IDEA WHAT THE WORLD *REALLY* WAS.

ON THE STREETS OF DOWNTOWN FRESNO, HE DIDN'T EVEN NOTICE...

...HOW EVERY MAN TURNED TO WATCH HER PASS BY.

EVERY MAN BUT *ONE*.

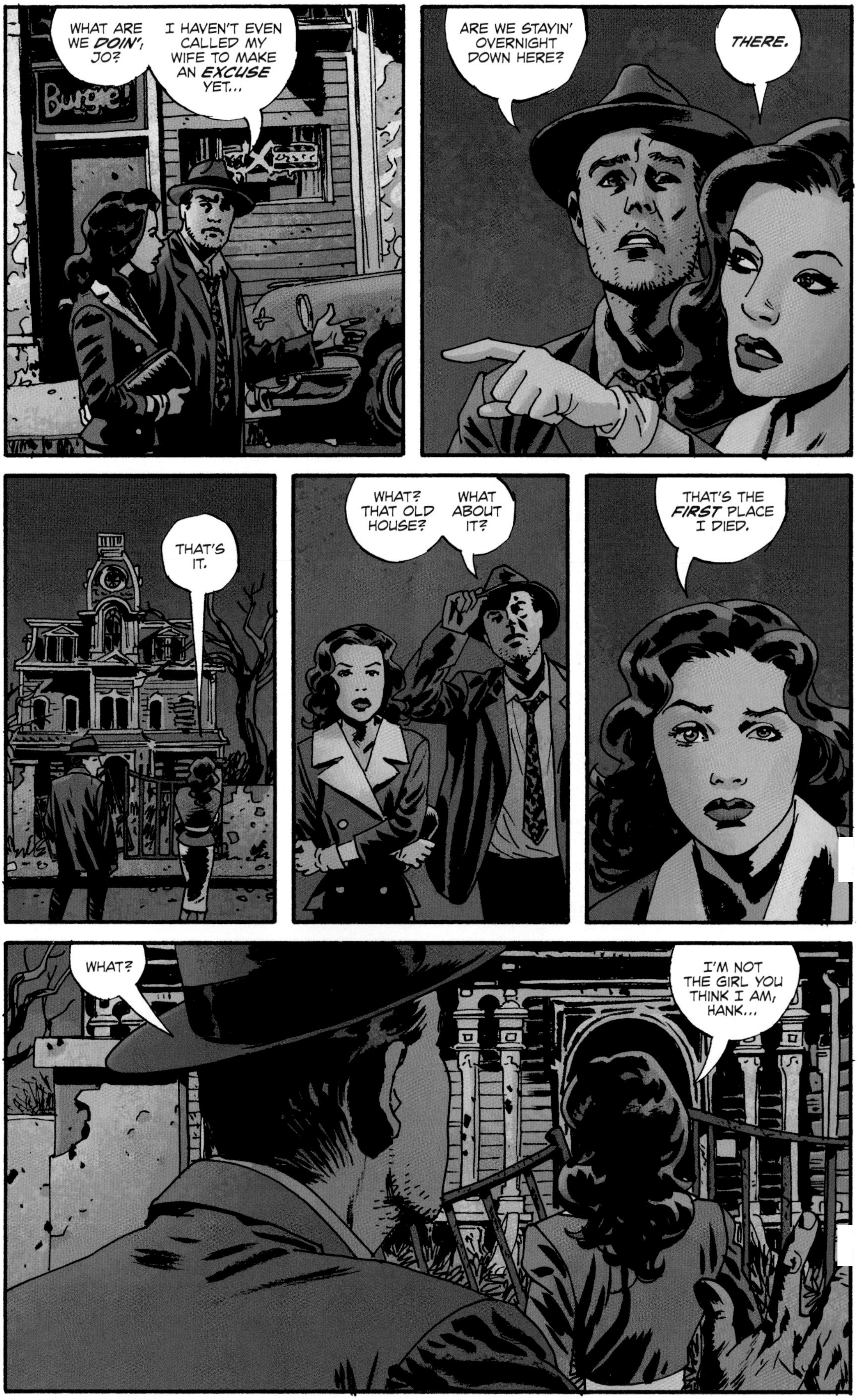
WHAT ARE WE *DOIN'*, JO?
I HAVEN'T EVEN CALLED MY WIFE TO MAKE AN *EXCUSE* YET...
ARE WE STAYIN' OVERNIGHT DOWN HERE?
THERE.
THAT'S IT.
WHAT? THAT OLD HOUSE?
WHAT ABOUT IT?
THAT'S THE *FIRST* PLACE I DIED.
WHAT?
I'M NOT THE GIRL YOU THINK I AM, HANK...

HEY... IS THAT SOME KINDA JOKE?

THE *GIRLS* WHO LIVED HERE... WITH THEIR BOOZE AND THEIR PARTIES...

YOU'D HEAR THE MUSIC FROM A *BLOCK* AWAY...

GOD... THEY WERE *SO* BEAUTIFUL.

THEY --

WHAT? WHAT IS IT?

SOMEONE'S INSIDE. I SAW A SHADOW MOVING...

HANG ON... I'LL CHECK IT OUT.

IT'S PROBABLY *NOTHING.*

SHE WAITS A FEW MOMENTS, CURSING HERSELF...

...BECAUSE SHE KNOWS IT'S *NOT* NOTHING.

HANK?

DOWN HERE...

...AN' STILL BREATHIN' FOR NOW.

SHOULD I HIT 'IM AGAIN?

NO. YOU GET AWAY FROM HIM.

EASY... YOU DON'T NEED THAT...

I MEAN YOU NO HARM... NOT YOU...

NO... I PRAYED YOU MIGHT COME BACK THIS WAY SOMEDAY...

STAY BACK. I'M NOT KIDDING.

THING IS, WHEN YOU WENT BY BEFORE... IT'S LIKE I COULDN'T FOCUS...

LIKE YOU WAS A BLUR...

BUT I SEE YOU NOW.

NO!

SMAAK

AHH -- !

BET YOU DON'T EVEN REMEMBER ME...

I WAS BARELY A MAN... DIDN'T GET A TASTE...

BUT YOU REMEMBER *THESE*, I BET...

JUST LIKE THE ONES THE MASTER HAD.

I REMEMBER YOU.

REALLY?

YES. YOU WERE THE SCARED KID WHO *PISSED* HIMSELF.

DON'T MOCK. THAT WAS THE GREATEST NIGHT OF MY *LIFE*...

I'M HAVE NO DOUBT ABOUT THAT...

AND I'M *NOT* MOCKING. I DON'T REMEMBER ALL OF IT...

"...JUST FLASHES..."

"...AND NIGHTMARES..."

BUT HOW COULD I *EVER* FORGET YOUR BROKEN SMILE?

YOUR STUPID LAUGHTER... CRYING AND WAITING FOR YOUR *SICK GODS* TO ARRIVE...

THEY -- THEY *REMADE* YOU... MADE YOU *PERFECT*...

THEY MADE ME *SOMETHING*... THAT'S FOR SURE...

AND I KNEW YOU, OR SOMEONE *LIKE* YOU, WOULD BE HERE...

...GUARDING YOUR HOLY GROUND...

THAT'S WHY I MADE MY *FRIEND* COME IN FIRST... AS *BAIT*.

WUHH...

AND THAT'S WHY I *LET YOU* TAKE MY GUN...

WHAT...? I GOT...

NOW YOU CAN SEE *FIRSTHAND* WHAT THEY TURNED ME INTO.

JO...?

I WANT YOU TO TAKE THAT GUN...

AND *USE IT* TO GO SEE YOUR MASTER...

...WHAT... BUT... BUT...

YOU DON'T WANT THIS LIFE ANYWAY, RIGHT? IT'S JUST PAIN AND WAITING...

Y-YEAH... I DON'T...

THEN GO... FEEL THEIR ARMS *COIL* AROUND YOU...

...GO TO HELL.

JO!!

JESUS -- JO... WHAT...?

I TOLD YOU ...

I'M *NOT* THE GIRL YOU THINK I AM.

WHAT DID YOU -- DID YOU *DO* THIS?

STOP. HE'S *DEAD...* YOU'RE JUST GETTING HIS *BLOOD* EVERYWHERE.

WE HAVE TO CALL THE POLICE... WE...

OH GOD... JESUS...

COME ON, HANK. WE'RE LEAVING...

SO PULL YOURSELF TOGETHER.

SHE'S CRAZY, HANK THINKS. *SHE'S A MONSTER.*

AND THAT'S *BEFORE* SHE LIGHTS THE PLACE ON FIRE.

AFTER THAT HE JUST FEELS DOOMED.

HE SPENDS HALF THE DRIVE BACK TO SAN FRANCISCO TERRIFIED, HIS MIND RACING...

WHY DID HE GO INTO THAT HOUSE?

WHAT THE HELL DID JOSEPHINE *DO* TO THAT MAN?

BUT SOMEWHERE ON THE ROAD, A *CALM* COMES OVER HIM...

ALMOST OUT OF NOWHERE.

ALMOST LIKE MAGIC.

BY THE TIME THEY REACH THE CITY, HE'S ACTUALLY CONVINCED SHE SAVED HIM FROM A CRAZED HOBO *KILLER.*

ALL HANK IS WORRYING ABOUT IS THE LIE HE'LL HAVE TO TELL HIS WIFE...

...UNTIL HE SEES THE CLUSTER OF *POLICE* OUTSIDE HIS HOME.

WHAT THE HELL...?

--SAID SHE WAS *PREGNANT,* TOO.

CHRIST...

STEP BACK. POLICE BUSINESS.

WHAT'S GOING ON HERE?

IS THAT *BLOOD* ON YOUR SHIRT?

LET ME *THROUGH.* THAT'S MY HOUSE, MY --

HEY!

THAT'S THE *HUSBAND!* HOLD HIM!

WHAT?! HEY, *STOP* - HEY!

LET GO!

WHAT IS THIS?! *WHAT IS THIS?!!*

YOU'RE *UNDER ARREST,* YOU SICK FUCK...

Chapter Four

SOMETHING WOKE "MAYDAY" LUCCARELLI IN THE MIDDLE OF THE NIGHT.

HE THOUGHT MAYBE THE HOUSE HAD BEEN SHAKING.

LIKE AN *EARTHQUAKE*.

BUT WHATEVER IT WAS, HE WAS PISSED.

...WHAT THE FUCK...?

HE HAD A MEETING WITH THAT PRICK *POLICE LIEUTENANT* FOR THE MORNING...

...AND HIS LAWYER SAID HE COULDN'T MISS IT. NOT AFTER GETTING HIS *PICTURE* IN THE PAPER...

HEY... DANNY?

WITH THOSE STUPID FUCKING COPS, BOOKER AND DALTON.

BRUNO? GUYS?

IF HE HAD TO *GIVE THEM UP* TO STAY OUT OF JAIL, THEN *SO BE IT...*

YOU GUYS *FEEL* THAT?

OH YES... THEY *DEFINITELY* FELT SOMETHING.

JESUS!

WHAT THE HELL DID YOU --?!

WHO *ARE* YOU?!

THEY CALL ME MR BISHOP... AND I'M ACTUALLY A *BIG FAN* OF YOUR'S...

I MEAN, YOU'RE ONE *COLD BASTARD,* MAYDAY...

WHAT -- WHAT THE FUCK DO YOU PEOPLE *WANT?!*

SADLY, NOTHING...

IT'S JUST THAT *YOUR* PLANS AND *MINE* ARE AT CROSS PURPOSES.

YOU UNDERSTAND WHAT *THAT'S* LIKE, *RIGHT?*

JOSEPHINE DIDN'T KNOW WHAT SHE WAS DOING.

IT HAD BEEN A MISTAKE, SHOWING HANK THE TRUTH... EVEN IF HE DIDN'T UNDERSTAND IT.

BUT THAT HOUSE NEEDED TO BE BURNED.

TO ERASE WHATEVER POWER IT HELD OVER HER... THAT AWFUL PLACE.

AND YET, HERE SHE WAS, NOT FEELING *MORE* POWERFUL...

BUT LOOKING FOR A *BACK-UP* PLAN... BEING STUPID.

FEELING LIKE IT WAS ALL GOING *WRONG*...

BECAUSE, OF COURSE... IT WAS.

THE DETECTIVE HAD SPENT OVER AN HOUR TRYING TO GET HANK TO CONFESS.

THEN SOMEONE ARRIVED WITH PICTURES FROM THE CRIME SCENE...

...AND HE WAS FORCED TO LOOK AT WHAT WAS LEFT OF HIS WIFE.

WHICH WASN'T MUCH.

THEN THEY TOLD HIM THE BABY HAD BEEN CUT OUT OF HER... BEFORE IT WAS RIPPED APART.

THAT WAS WHEN HE STARTED SCREAMING.

HE DOESN'T REMEMBER WHEN HE STOPPED.

SO, WHAT DO WE *THINK*...?

HE'S HIDING *SOMETHIN'*... BUT I DON'T THINK HE'S OUR MAN ON THIS.

NO ONE'S *THAT* GOOD AN ACTOR.

WHAT ABOUT THE *BLOOD* ON HIS SHIRT AND JACKET?

YOU SAW THAT *SCENE*, LIEUTENANT... HE WOULDN'T JUST HAVE A FEW SPOTS.

WELL, DON'T LOOK AT ME AND LANNIE.

YEAH, JUST 'CAUSE THAT SHITHEEL PUT US ON THE *FRONT PAGE* DOESN'T MEAN WE *RETURNED* THE FAVOR.

JESUS CHRIST, DALTON...

WHAT? I'M SUPPOSED TO *LIKE HIM* NOW 'CAUSE SOMEONE *HACKED UP* HIS WIFE?

THE LIEUTENANT ALREADY CONFIRMED YOU WERE BOTH *WITH HIM* AT THE TIME OF THE MURDER...

...BUT THAT *DOESN'T* MEAN YOU AREN'T INVOLVED.

STEP BACK, BUDDY.

I SAW THOSE CRIME SCENE PHOTOS, TOO...

...AN' I'LL KNOCK YOUR LIGHTS OUT IF YOU SAY THAT *AGAIN*.

YEAH? I'D LIKE TO SEE YOU TRY.

ENOUGH OF THIS HORSESHIT!

TELL THEM WHAT YOU TOLD ME, WOODSON.

RIGHT... GOT A CALL FROM A NEIGHBOR...

SAYS HE SAW THREE MEN LEAVING THE RAINES RESIDENCE YESTERDAY.

DESCRIPTIONS MATCH YOUR PAL "MAYDAY" AND HIS CREW.

AND LUCCARELLI DIDN'T SHOW FOR HIS INTERVIEW TODAY.

NO SIGN OF HIM AT ANY OF HIS RESIDENCES...

LOOKS LIKE HE'S ON THE RUN.

WAIT, YOU THINK WE GOT LUCCARELLI TO WHACK THIS REPORTER'S WIFE?

AND WHY WOULD HE EVEN *DO* THAT?

THE MAN'S A *MOBSTER*, BOOKER...

THEIR REACTIONS AREN'T *EXACTLY* KNOWN TO BE CIVILIZED.

AHH, THE *HELL* WITH THIS...

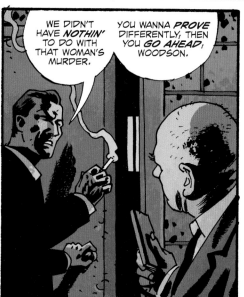

WE DIDN'T HAVE *NOTHIN'* TO DO WITH THAT WOMAN'S MURDER.

YOU WANNA *PROVE* DIFFERENTLY, THEN YOU *GO AHEAD*, WOODSON.

UNTIL YOU *DO*, WE GOT OUR *OWN* HOMICIDES TO WORK...

SO GO FUCK YOURSELF.

HOU CE

SLAAAM

WELL, THAT WENT ABOUT AS I EXPECTED...

YOU THINK THEY'RE INVOLVED?

THOSE TWO ARE DIRTY AS HELL... BUT SOMETHING LIKE THIS...?

"EVEN *THEY* AREN'T THAT SICK..."

GRRAAA --!

...UUHK...

WALT FELT LIKE KILLING HIMSELF...

...WHICH HE KNEW WAS *EXACTLY* WHAT THE DEMON WANTED.

GOD DAMN IT...

HAD HE *REALLY* NOT BEEN PAYING ATTENTION...

...WHEN IT TOLD HIM THERE WOULD BE A *PRICE*?

WHAT HAVE YOU *DONE,* WALTER...?

YOU FOOLISH SELFISH MAN...

JO...? *HOW*...? WHAT'RE YOU DOIN' HERE?

HOW -- HOW DID YOU GET PAST THE DESK SERGEANT?

HOW DO *YOU* THINK?

I NEEDED TO SEE YOU.

THOUGHT I WAS THE *LAST THING* YOU WANTED TO SEE.

STOP IT.

I *HAD* TO PROTECT MYSELF.

SO YOU RUN OFF WITH THAT... THAT...

GOD, I COULD PRACTICALLY *SMELL YOU* ON HIM.

YES. AND I SAW IN THE PAPER WHAT *HAPPENED* TO HIS WIFE...

I DIDN'T...

YOU KNOW THAT'S *NOTHING* COMPARED TO WHAT THEY'LL DO TO ME.

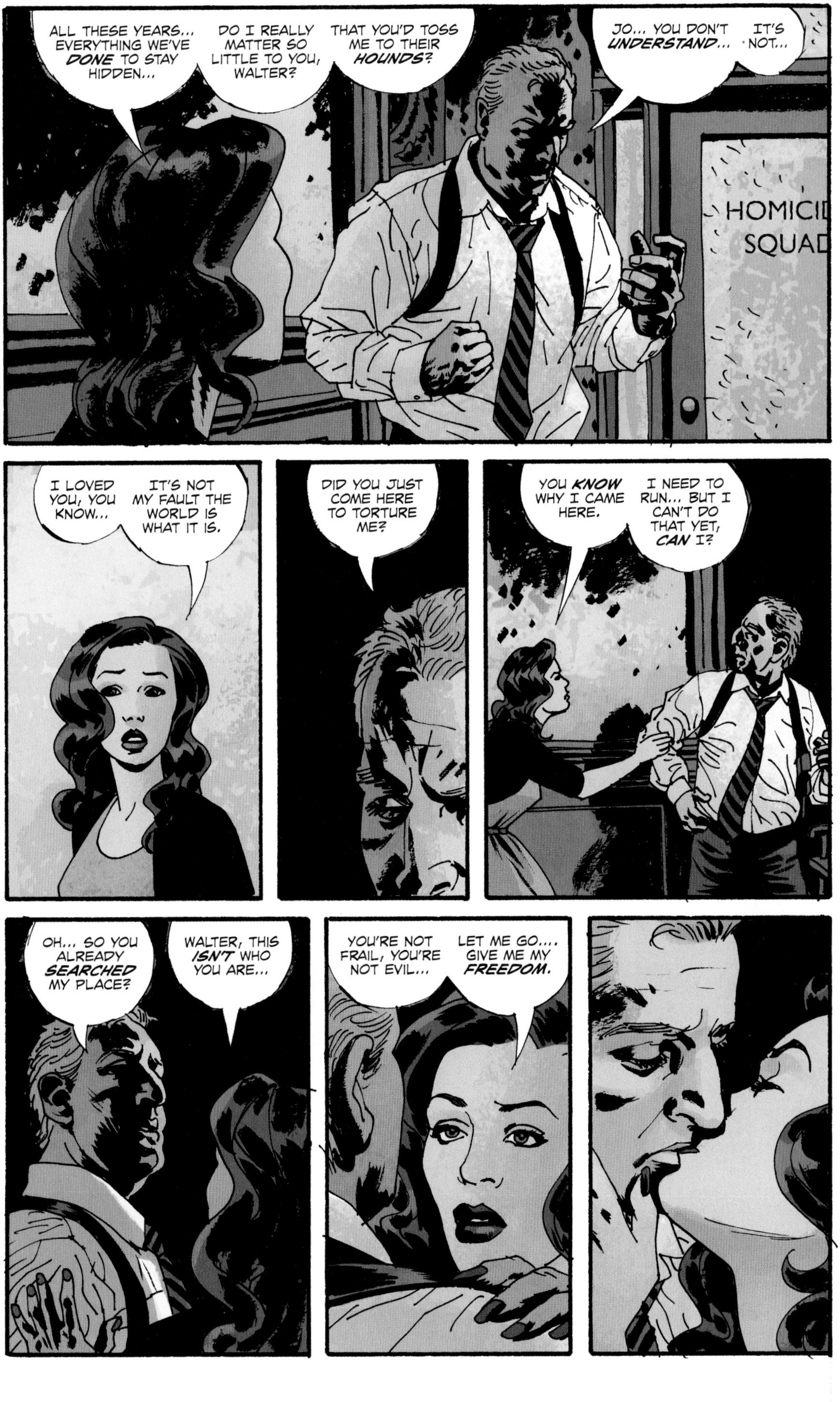
ALL THESE YEARS... EVERYTHING WE'VE DONE TO STAY HIDDEN...
DO I REALLY MATTER SO LITTLE TO YOU, WALTER?
THAT YOU'D TOSS ME TO THEIR HOUNDS?
JO... YOU DON'T UNDERSTAND...
IT'S NOT...
HOMICID
SQUAD
I LOVED YOU, YOU KNOW...
IT'S NOT MY FAULT THE WORLD IS WHAT IT IS.
DID YOU JUST COME HERE TO TORTURE ME?
YOU KNOW WHY I CAME HERE.
I NEED TO RUN... BUT I CAN'T DO THAT YET, CAN I?
OH... SO YOU ALREADY SEARCHED MY PLACE?
WALTER, THIS ISN'T WHO YOU ARE...
YOU'RE NOT FRAIL, YOU'RE NOT EVIL...
LET ME GO.... GIVE ME MY FREEDOM.

OKAY... OKAY...

I CAN'T GET TO IT UNTIL THE MORNING, THOUGH...

TOMORROW THEN... WE'LL MEET AT THE *CLIFF HOUSE*.

SURE. LIKE THE OLD DAYS.

EXCEPT IN THE OLD DAYS, I WASN'T RUNNING FOR MY LIFE.

YOU DON'T *GET* IT...

THEY WERE ALREADY *HERE*, I WASN'T --

DON'T LET ME DOWN, WALTER... PLEASE...

THE PROBLEM WAS, WALTER BOOKER HAD *NEVER* BEEN LIKE OTHER PEOPLE.

EVEN AS A CHILD, HE'D SEEN PIECES OF THE WORLD HE WASN'T MEANT TO.

ONCE HE'D TOLD HIS MOTHER THERE WERE OTHER LAYERS TO REALITY; *HIDDEN* ONES...

WHERE GHOSTS AND MONSTERS, AND EVEN ANGELS OF A SORT, MOVED IN SHADOW.

AND AN UNSEEN CLOCKWORK THAT MADE THE UNIVERSE TICK.

BUT HE COULD TELL EVEN AS HE WAS EXPLAINING...

THAT SHE COULD NEVER UNDERSTAND.

THAT SHE COULD NEVER SEE THE THINGS HE SAW WITH THE CORNERS OF HIS EYES.

IT HAD HELPED HIM SURVIVE THE WAR, THAT SIGHT.

AND IT HAD LED HIM TO JOSEPHINE.

IT HAD EVEN MADE HIM A BETTER COP, FOR A WHILE.

BUT IT WORE HIM DOWN, KNOWING HOW SMALL HE WAS...

HOW INSIGNIFICANT HE WAS TO THE THINGS IN THE SHADOWS...

IT WORE HIM DOWN UNTIL THERE WAS SO LITTLE LEFT IN HIM...

...THAT HE *ALMOST* FORGOT WHO HE REALLY WAS.

HOMICID
SQUAD

HANK HAD NO IDEA HOW LONG HE'D BEEN *HELD* WHEN THEY LET HIM GO...

...BUT HIS FRIEND JOHNNY LASH WAS *WAITING.*

HANK!

JESUS! YOU *OKAY?*

... I DON'T... I...

IT'S OKAY, PAL... I GOT YOU...

SO, HE'S *FREE* FOR NOW, BUT MAKE SURE HE DOESN'T LEAVE TOWN.

YOU SON OF A BITCH...

YOU *KNOW* HE HAD *NOTHIN'* TO DO WITH THIS.

YOU SO SURE ABOUT THAT, SONNY? ME, I THINK YOUR PAL'S *DEEP* INTO SOMETHIN'...

...I'M JUST NOT SURE *WHAT...* YET.

SO LOOK... YOU'RE STAYIN' WITH ME AND PENNY UNTIL THIS IS OVER...

OKAY?

BUT IT WASN'T OKAY.

HANK WAS DESTROYED, INSIDE AND OUT, BUT STILL....

I NEED... I NEED TO SEE JOSEPHINE...

ISSION POLICE STATION.

...ALL HE WANTED WAS TO CURL UP IN JO'S ARMS SO SHE COULD MAKE IT ALL BETTER.

AH, HANK, C'MON... DON'T BE AN IDIOT.

I NEED TO SEE HER...

EVEN THOUGH HE *KNEW* THAT WASN'T WHAT SHE DID.

PLEASE, JOHNNY...

SYLVIA IS *DEAD* -- YOUR WIFE!

SHOW SOME FRIGGIN' *RESPECT!*

...

LOOK... LET'S JUST GET A *DRINK*, OKAY...?

YOU'RE NOT YOURSELF...

SURE, SURE... THANKS, JOHNNY...

DETECTIVE BOOKER?

YEAH?

I HAVE A REPORT FROM THE *M.E.* FOR YOU...

ON *WHAT?*

THE *VICTIM* IN YOUR HOMICIDE?

VICTIM...? OH, THE *HANGED MAN?*

YES, I THINK THAT'S WHAT THE REPORT SAYS...

HUNG BY *ONE ANKLE*, STABBED *AND* BEATEN...

THEY *GET* SOMETHING ON HIM?

YES, AN *I.D.*

SOMEONE FROM HIS JOB FINALLY FILED A *MISSING PERSONS.*

WHAT -- *REALLY*?

IT'S ALL IN THERE.

THANKS, DAISY...

HEY, JAKE... YOU SEEN *LANNIE* AROUND?

NOT SINCE BEFORE LUNCH... *WHY*?

GOT A LEAD. IN OUR *CULT* MASSACRE.

SORRY...

AH... FUCK IT...

WALT WAS JUST HAPPY TO HAVE A DISTRACTION FROM HIS OWN PROBLEMS.

GO WORK THE CASE, HE TOLD HIMSELF.

HE DIDN'T WORRY MUCH ABOUT WHERE HIS PARTNER WAS...

TWO MORE OF THESE... AN' KEEP 'EM COMIN'...

...OR WHAT HE MIGHT BE *DOING.*

...AND WHY DID YOU WAIT SO LONG TO REPORT LEROY AS MISSING?

Garry's DINER

I JUST THOUGHT MAYBE HE WAS *SICK*...

BUT THEN I SAW THIS GIRL HE USED TO *DATE* IN HERE THIS MORNING...

SEEMED LIKE *SHE* WAS LOOKING FOR HIM, TOO... AND I JUST GOT *WORRIED.*

WITH GOOD REASON, TOO... POOR LEROY...

I'M *SORRY* ABOUT YOUR FRIEND...

BUT DO YOU KNOW WHERE CAN I FIND THIS WOMAN?

OH... ALL I REMEMBER IS SHE'S GOT ONE OF *THOSE* NAMES...

LIKE THAT WORKS FOR A BOY OR A GIRL... LIKE SAM...

...OR MAYBE *JO.*

HANK COULDN'T GET THE IMAGES OUT OF HIS MIND...

THE BITS OF HER BODY, ALL TORN AND BLOODY.

OR THE COP'S ACCUSATIONS.

WAS THIS HIS FAULT, SOMEHOW?

HE EXPECTED STATIC FROM THE COPS, EVEN THREATS...

BUT SYLVIA LOOKED LIKE SHE'D BEEN ATTACKED BY... SOMETHING INHUMAN.

EVEN DRUNK, HE COULDN'T BELIEVE THE POLICE HAD DONE THAT.

AND YET, HE KEPT SEEING THE CRIME SCENE OVER AND OVER IN HIS HEAD...

KEPT FEELING MORE AND MORE TO BLAME...

JOHNNY WAS TRYING TO DO THE RIGHT THING, TO TAKE CARE OF HIS BEST FRIEND...

BUT HE DIDN'T UNDERSTAND. HE COULDN'T.

HANK WAS ONLY BEGINNING TO UNDERSTAND HIMSELF...

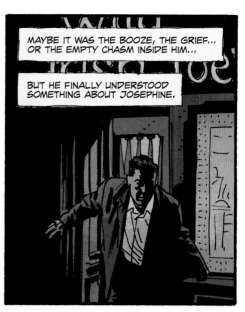

MAYBE IT WAS THE BOOZE, THE GRIEF... OR THE EMPTY CHASM INSIDE HIM...

BUT HE FINALLY UNDERSTOOD SOMETHING ABOUT JOSEPHINE.

AND HE CRAVED HER BECAUSE OF IT.

BECAUSE SHE COULD MAKE HIM *STOP* SEEING HIS DEAD WIFE...

HANK?

HEY, DID YOU SEE WHERE MY FRIEND WENT?

SORRY.

AND WHAT WAS LEFT OF THE *SON* THEY ALMOST HAD...

...SHIT...

WHICH WASN'T MUCH...

WHAT...?

WRONG WAY, SHITBIRD!

AHH -- !

JESUS!

NOW LISTEN HERE, BUDDY. I KNOW YOU BEEN THROUGH HELL...

BUT UNLESS YOU WANNA *JOIN* YOUR WIFE THERE PERMANENTLY...

YOU'RE GONNA *TELL ME* WHO TIPPED YOU TO OUR MEET WITH *LUCCARELLI*...

WHAT--*WHAT*...?!

TELL ME WHO *SET US UP!*

KRAAK

GAAH--!

JO. THIS FUCKING MANIAC WAS AFTER JOSEPHINE.

...WAS A... *TIP...* SOMEONE CALLED IN...

DON'T GIMME THAT CHICKENSHIT...

WAIT A *SEC*...

WHAT?

AND HE HAD LED HIM *RIGHT* TO HER.

...WHERE THE *HELL* WERE YOU *GOIN'*...?

NOWHERE... I WASN'T –

WELL, LET'S JUST *SEE*. HOW 'BOUT THAT?

MOVE.

HANK'S MIND RACED DESPERATELY...

HE WAS DRUNK, AND *NOT* A FIGHTER...

BUT HE COULDN'T PUT JO IN THIS LUNATIC'S GRASP...

THERE HAD TO BE SOMETHING –

SHHK

SHHKK

HUU --

SHHKK SHKK

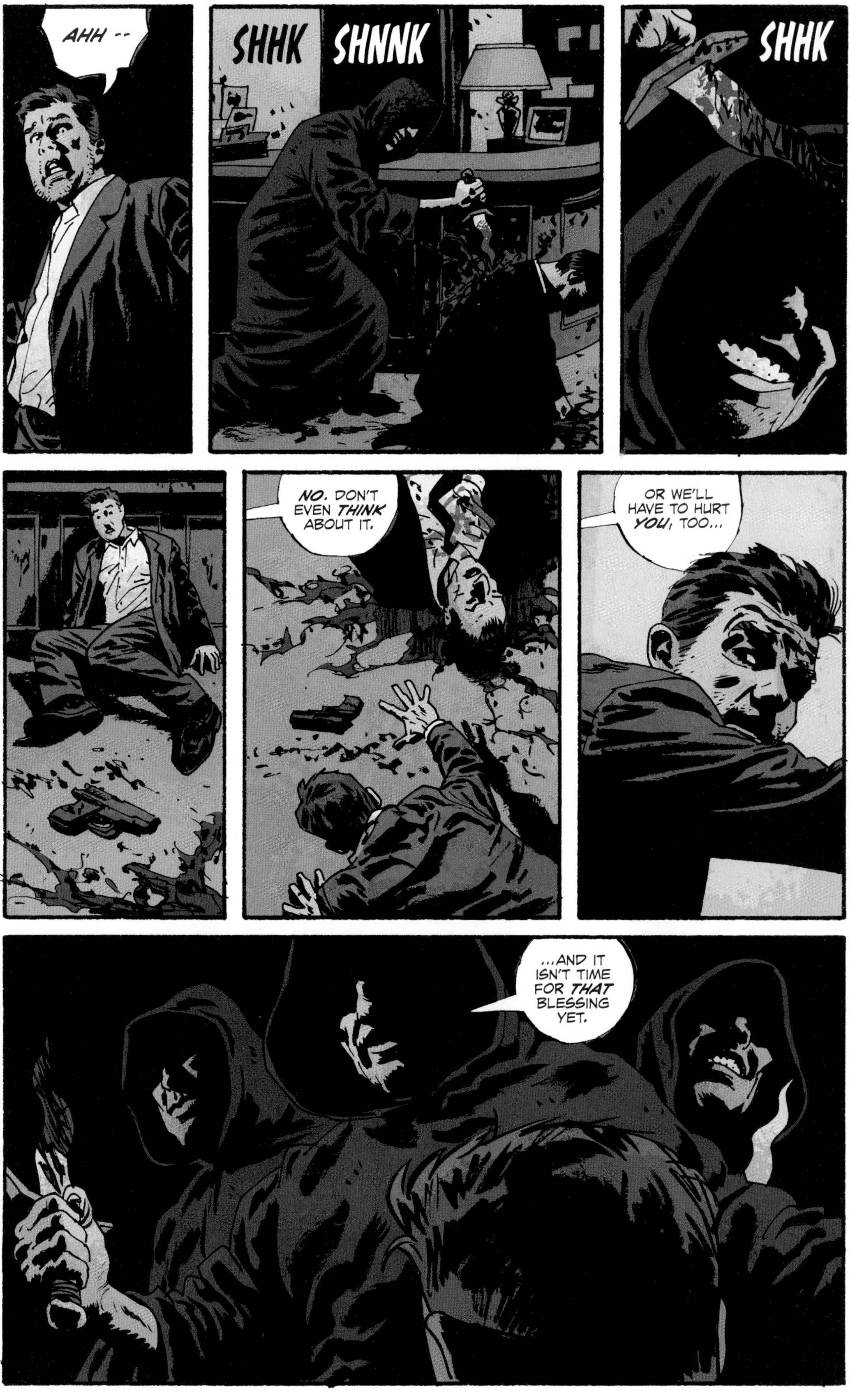
AHH --
SHHK
SHNNK
SHHK
NO. DON'T EVEN THINK ABOUT IT.
OR WE'LL HAVE TO HURT YOU, TOO...
...AND IT ISN'T TIME FOR THAT BLESSING YET.

Chapter
Five

WALTER FELT HIS SHIRT STICK TO THE BLOOD ON HIS ARM WHEN HE GOT OUT OF THE CAR.

THE WOUNDS SHOULD'VE BEEN DRY BY NOW.

HE HADN'T CARVED TOO DEEPLY.

IT MUST BE HIS DISEASE.

JUST BEFORE THE RITUAL, HE'D COUGHED UP MORE BLOOD THAN HE THOUGHT POSSIBLE.

IT WAS SURPRISING HE COULD EVEN WALK RIGHT THEN...

...BUT HE'D NEED *MUCH* MORE STRENGTH TO DO WHAT HE HAD TO.

COFFEE SHOP

JOSEPHINE FELT FEVERISH AND SICK... EVEN EDGY.

SHE WASN'T USED TO THAT, NOT SINCE THE EARLY DAYS OF HER NEW LIFE.

BUT LAST NIGHT THERE'D BEEN POLICE AT HER HOTEL, CORDONING OFF A *CRIME SCENE* IN THE LOBBY.

AND TODAY SHE COULDN'T FIND HANK, OR *FEEL HIM* IN HER THOUGHTS.

SHE DIDN'T EVEN KNOW WHY SHE'D COME HERE...

WHY SHE'D TRUST THAT WALTER –

OH!

YOU'RE HERE... I...

I SAID I'D MEET YOU.

BUT SHE HADN'T FELT HIM APPROACHING.

YES...

SHE USED TO SENSE HIM... LIKE HE WAS A PHANTOM, LINKED TO HER.

SO... YOU HAVE THE...?

YEAH.

I WAS ONLY *EVER* KEEPIN' IT FOR YOU...

HAVE -- DID YOU *TRANSLATE* ANY *MORE*?

NO...

BUT HE'D STARED AT IT SO LONG THAT HE NEARLY LOST HIS MIND...

AN UNSPOKEN LANGUAGE WRITTEN ON THE SKIN OF SOME ANCIENT WYRM...

HE'D TAKEN IT AND *ONE OTHER THING* FROM THE ALTAR THAT DAY...

THE DAY HE *SAVED* JOSEPHINE THE FIRST TIME...

SO, WHAT WAS THE *PLAN*, JO?

YOUR *REPORTER* MAKES MY LIFE HELL, AN' WHILE I'M DISTRACTED...

YOU GET YOUR HANDS ON *THAT* AN' THE TWO OF YOU RACE THE SUNSET?

ESSENTIALLY... YES.

BUT YOU CAN *NEVER* COUNT ON PLANS...

OR *I* CAN'T, AT LEAST.

AND HOW DID *LEROY KRESSLER* FIT INTO YOUR PLANS?

WHAT? HOW DO YOU KNOW ABOUT...?

BECAUSE I'M *WORKIN'* HIS MURDER...

WHICH WAS A *RITUAL SACRIFICE.*

...WHAT...?

TRIED TO TELL YOU I *DIDN'T* SUMMON THEM, THEY WERE *ALREADY* HERE.

AN' IT WASN'T A *COINCIDENCE* I GOT THAT CASE.

THEY WERE *LOOKIN'* FOR ME.

SOMEHOW THEY'RE TRACKING YOUR SCENT.

OH GOD, *HANK*.

THE NAME STABS WHAT'S LEFT OF HIS HEART.

I COULDN'T FIND HIM... HE'S MISSING - HE -

HEY.

WALTER... IS THAT *BLOOD* ON YOUR SLEEVE?

AND HE HOLDS ONTO THAT FEELING.

YES.

KRAAK

DON'T WORRY... I'LL TAKE YOU TO HIM.

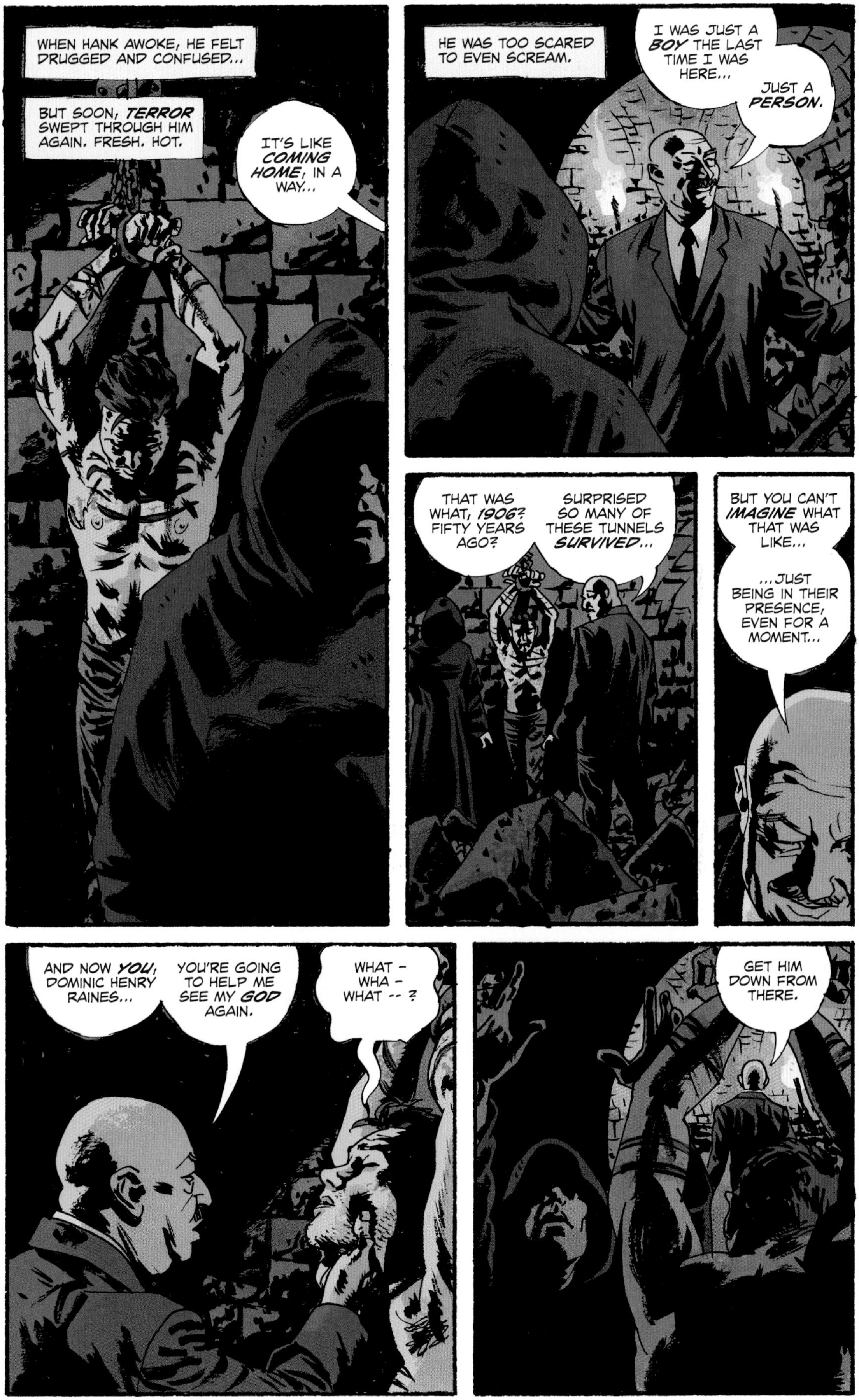
WHEN HANK AWOKE, HE FELT DRUGGED AND CONFUSED...
BUT SOON, TERROR SWEPT THROUGH HIM AGAIN. FRESH. HOT.
IT'S LIKE COMING HOME, IN A WAY...
HE WAS TOO SCARED TO EVEN SCREAM.
I WAS JUST A BOY THE LAST TIME I WAS HERE...
JUST A PERSON.
THAT WAS WHAT, 1906? FIFTY YEARS AGO?
SURPRISED SO MANY OF THESE TUNNELS SURVIVED...
BUT YOU CAN'T IMAGINE WHAT THAT WAS LIKE...
...JUST BEING IN THEIR PRESENCE, EVEN FOR A MOMENT...
AND NOW YOU, DOMINIC HENRY RAINES...
YOU'RE GOING TO HELP ME SEE MY GOD AGAIN.
WHAT - WHA - WHAT -- ?
GET HIM DOWN FROM THERE.

I WANT YOU TO UNDERSTAND HOW LUCKY YOU ARE, RAINES...

YOU'VE STEPPED AWAY FROM THE RABBLE...

THANKS TO YOUR WOMAN.

ALTHOUGH *YOU* WON'T BE THANKING HER, I'M SURE.

WH -- WHERE... WHERE ARE WE...?

UNDERNEATH YOUR CITY.

IN ITS *BOWELS.*

THIS IS WHERE HER *PREDECESSOR* DIED, WHEN SAN FRANCISCO NEARLY FELL INTO THE SEA...

HEH HEH...

GOD, WHAT A GLORIOUS DAY *THAT* WAS.

...I DON'T... YOU SAID 1906...?

WHO... WHO *ARE* YOU...?

WHAT'RE YOU *TALKING* ABOUT...?

SACRIFICE, RAINES... I'M TALKING ABOUT A *SACRIFICE!*

LIKE YOUR *WIFE* WAS.

MY...?

...WHO *ARE* YOU?

MR *BISHOP!*

HE'S HERE... BOOKER DID AS HE PROMISED.

GOOD.

PUT OUR GUEST IN HIS ROOM, UNTIL IT'S TIME.

YES, MY LORD...

WAIT — WAIT — YOU SAID BOOKER?

STOP! STOP! LET ME *GO!*

WALT FELT ELECTRIFIED. THE HIDDEN MARKINGS ON HIS ARMS WERE *PULSING*.

GOT A LIGHT?

NO.

GOD, HE HATED USING SPELLS.

WELL, SHIT...

SO, YOU MADE THE DEADLINE...

I HOPE SHE ISN'T *TOO* DAMAGED?

SEE FOR *YOURSELF*...

YEEESSSS... GET HER OUT.

GIVE HER.

HOLD IT. WE HAD A *DEAL*, BISHOP.

WHAT ABOUT MY *CURE*?

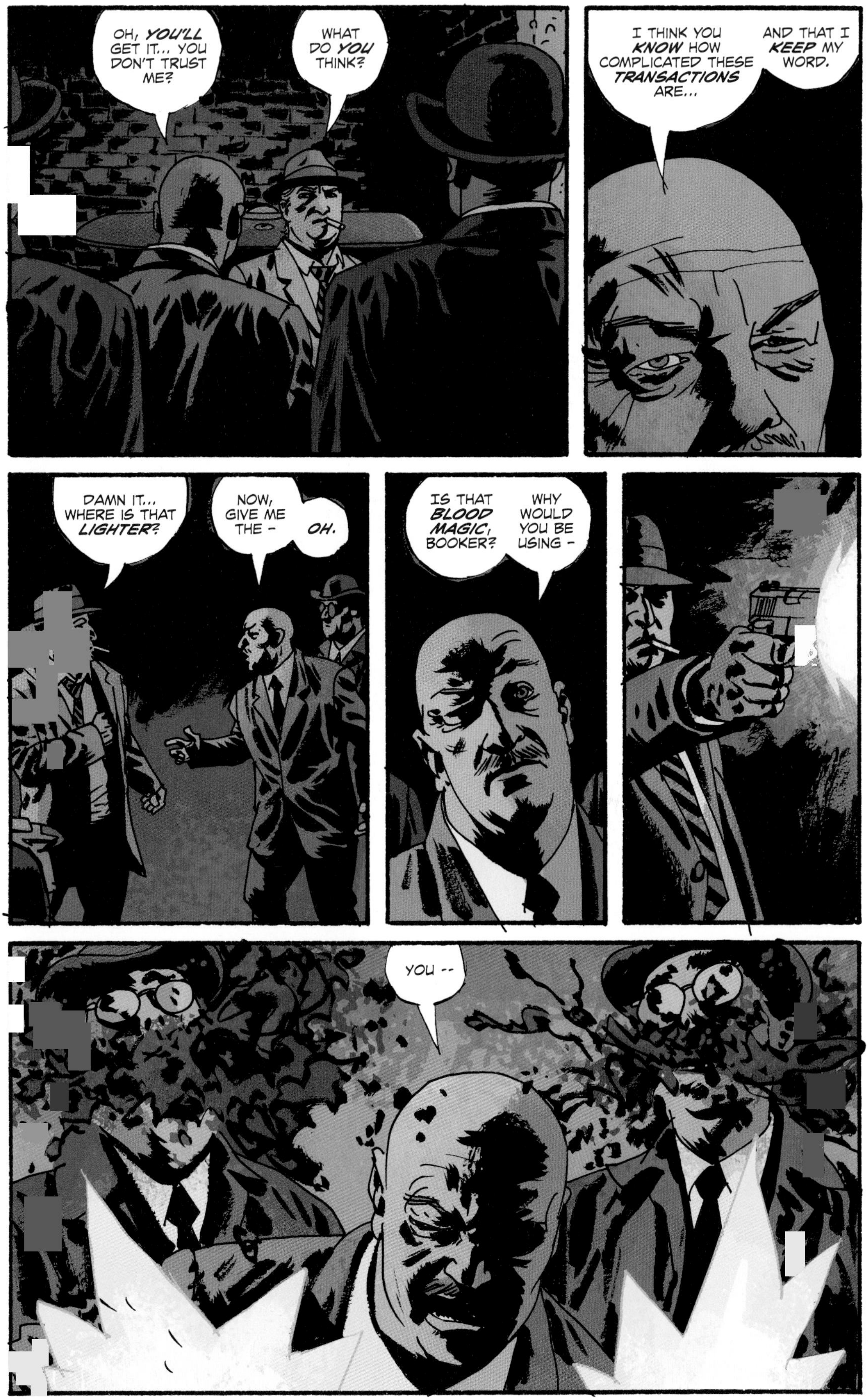
OH, *YOU'LL* GET IT... YOU DON'T TRUST ME?
WHAT DO *YOU* THINK?
I THINK YOU *KNOW* HOW COMPLICATED THESE *TRANSACTIONS* ARE...
AND THAT I *KEEP* MY WORD.
DAMN IT... WHERE IS THAT *LIGHTER*?
NOW, GIVE ME THE –
OH.
IS THAT *BLOOD MAGIC*, BOOKER?
WHY WOULD YOU BE USING –
YOU --

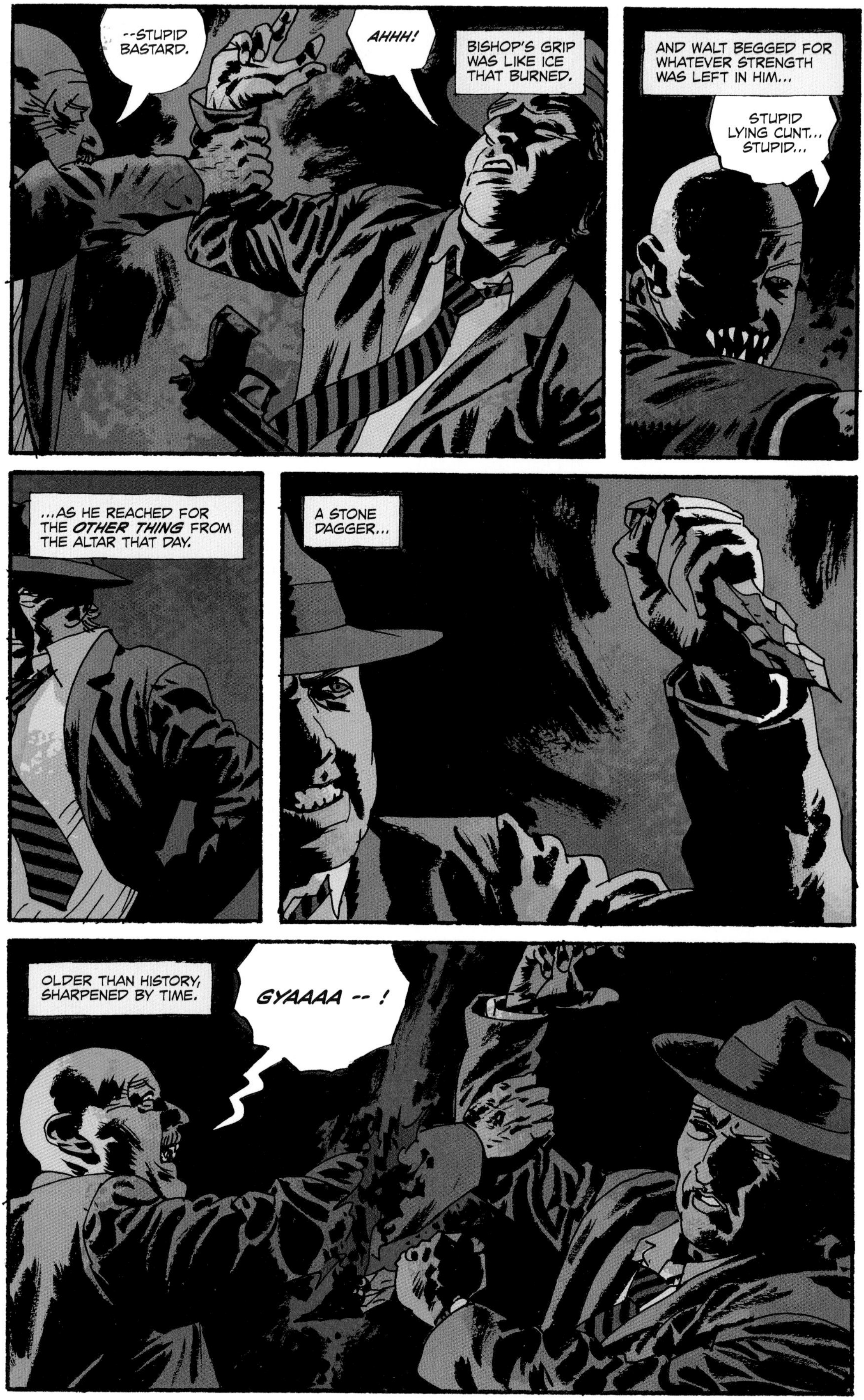
--STUPID BASTARD.
AHHH!
BISHOP'S GRIP WAS LIKE ICE THAT BURNED.
AND WALT BEGGED FOR WHATEVER STRENGTH WAS LEFT IN HIM...
STUPID LYING CUNT... STUPID...
...AS HE REACHED FOR THE OTHER THING FROM THE ALTAR THAT DAY.
A STONE DAGGER...
OLDER THAN HISTORY, SHARPENED BY TIME.
GYAAAA -- !

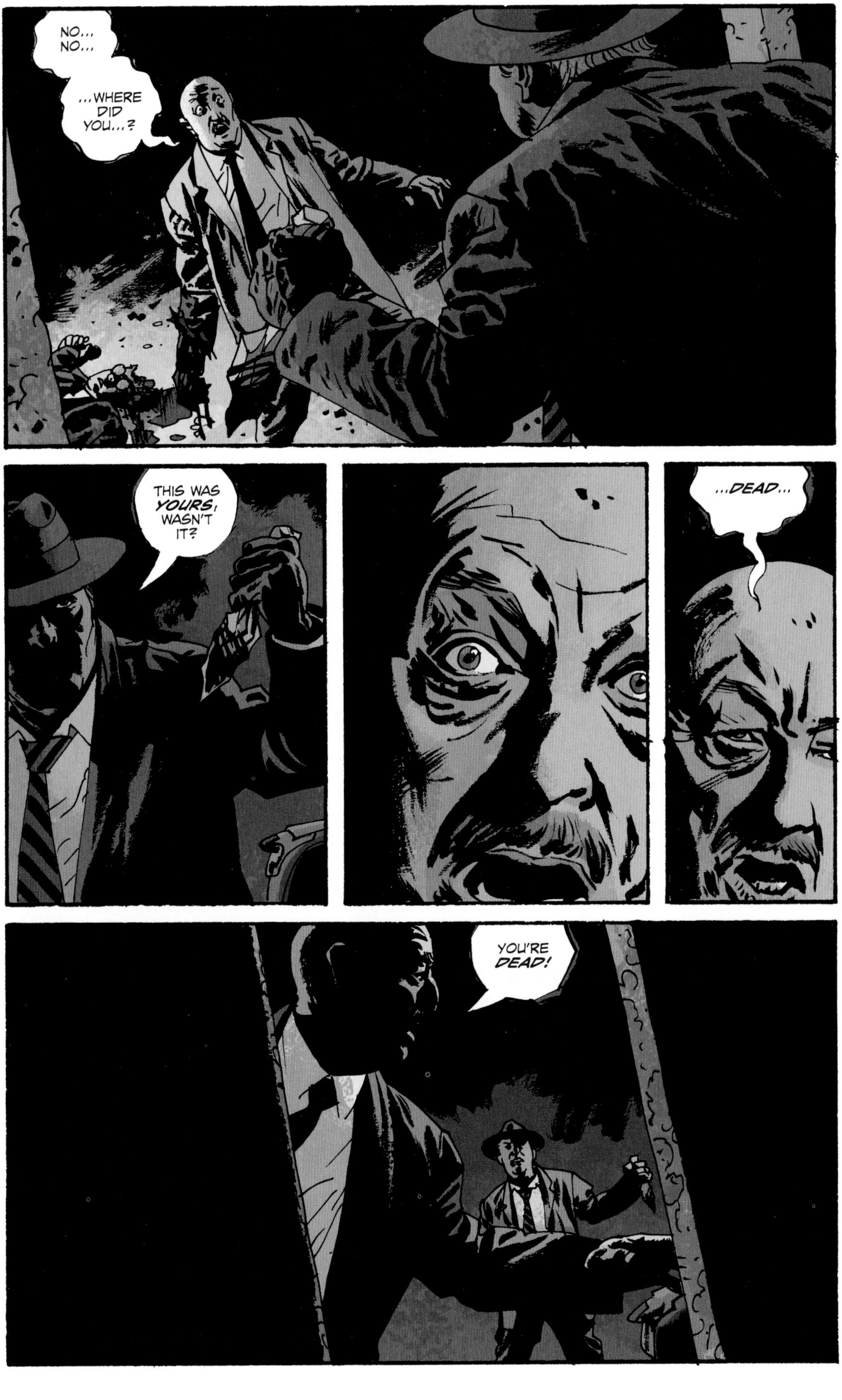
NO... NO...
...WHERE DID YOU...?
THIS WAS YOURS, WASN'T IT?
...DEAD...
YOU'RE DEAD!

CAREFUL... DON'T GET THAT THING'S *BLOOD* ON YOU.

I DON'T... WHAT ARE YOU...?

I MADE A PROMISE TO YOU ONCE...

DON'T HAVE MUCH TIME LEFT TO KEEP IT.

KEYS ARE IN THE *CAR.*

GET *OUTTA* HERE AND DON'T LOOK BACK...

...I'M GONNA FINISH THIS.

WAIT... DON'T –

BUT WALT WASN'T LISTENING, AND SHE DIDN'T REALLY WANT HIM TO STOP.

HE'D USED A *CURSE* TO SEVER THEIR BOND. CARVED HER OUT OF HIS HEART.

IT WAS THE ONLY WAY HE COULD USE HER LIKE HE HAD, TO LURE THE MONSTER.

BUT THEN IT GOT WORSE.

...NO...

SHE FELT *HANK'S* FEAR REACHING OUT TO HER...

...AND SHE CURSED HERSELF FOR THE THOUSANDTH TIME.

RUN! FUCKING *RUN,* SHITBIRDS!

GUUH -- !

BISHOP COULD HEAR THE ECHOED SCREAMS AND GUNFIRE...

BUT THE WORDS *HE* SPOKE MADE NO SOUND...

PRAYERS TO AN UNFORGIVING FATHER...

BEGGING FOR HIS GAZE TO FALL UPON HIM ONE MORE TIME...

OKAY, BISHOP...

...I GUESS WE'RE BOTH SHOWING OUR *TRUE FACES* NOW.

SOMETHING WAS WRONG, HANK 'NEW THAT.

HIS CAPTOR'S *PLANS* HAD GONE OFF THE RAILS... SOMEHOW.

AND THE GUNSHOTS WERE GETTING CLOSER.

WHAT THE HELL WAS HAPPENING?

HANK?

WHAT'VE THEY DONE TO YOU...?

NO, JO... YOU... YOU CAN'T BE HERE...

I *COULDN'T* LEAVE YOU HERE...

ALL OF THIS, *EVERYTHING*... IT'S MY --

THE *WOMAN!* IT'S THE *WOMAN!*

GET HER!

WALT SHOULDN'T HAVE BEEN *ABLE* TO WIELD THE KNIFE.

EACH TIME IT STRUCK, HE FELT HIS ARM WANTING TO CATCH FIRE.

BUT HE'D *MADE* HIS SACRIFICE.

LIKE BISHOP SAID, THERE WAS *ALWAYS* A COST.

FOOL... PRICK...

YOU CAN'T KILL ME...

I'M NOT *HERE*... TO KILL YOU...

BUT HE *TAKES* SOMETHING FROM THIS *CREATURE*...

...BEFORE HE TOSSES HIM INTO THE PIT.

AND THEN THE *EARTHQUAKE* BEGINS.

AHH, *SHIT!*

JO! LOOK OUT!

UNNH... *DAMN...* NNHH...

WAIT... IS IT OVER?

GIMME THAT...

HEY... I CAN'T --

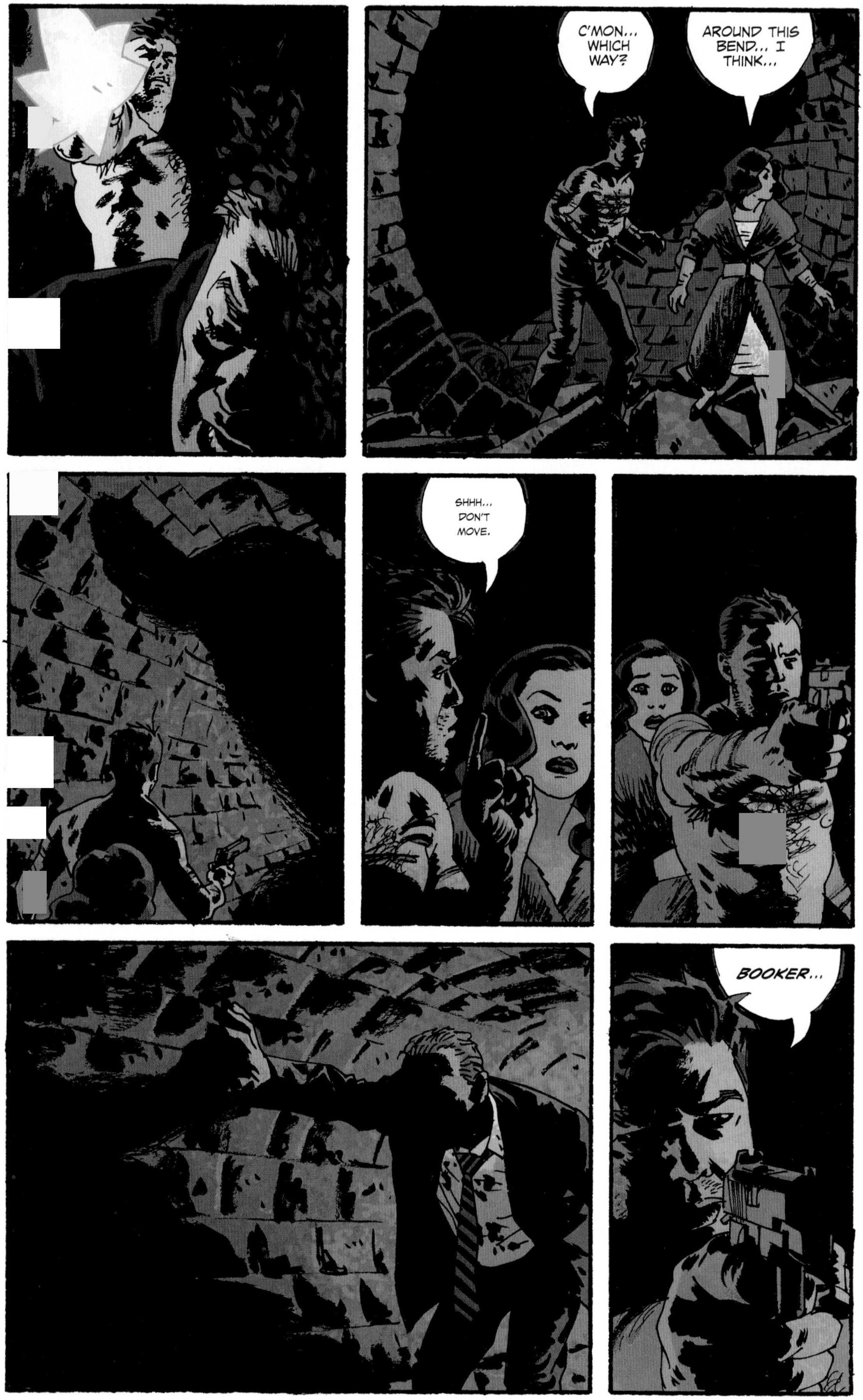
C'MON... WHICH WAY?
AROUND THIS BEND... I THINK...
SHHH... DON'T MOVE.
BOOKER...

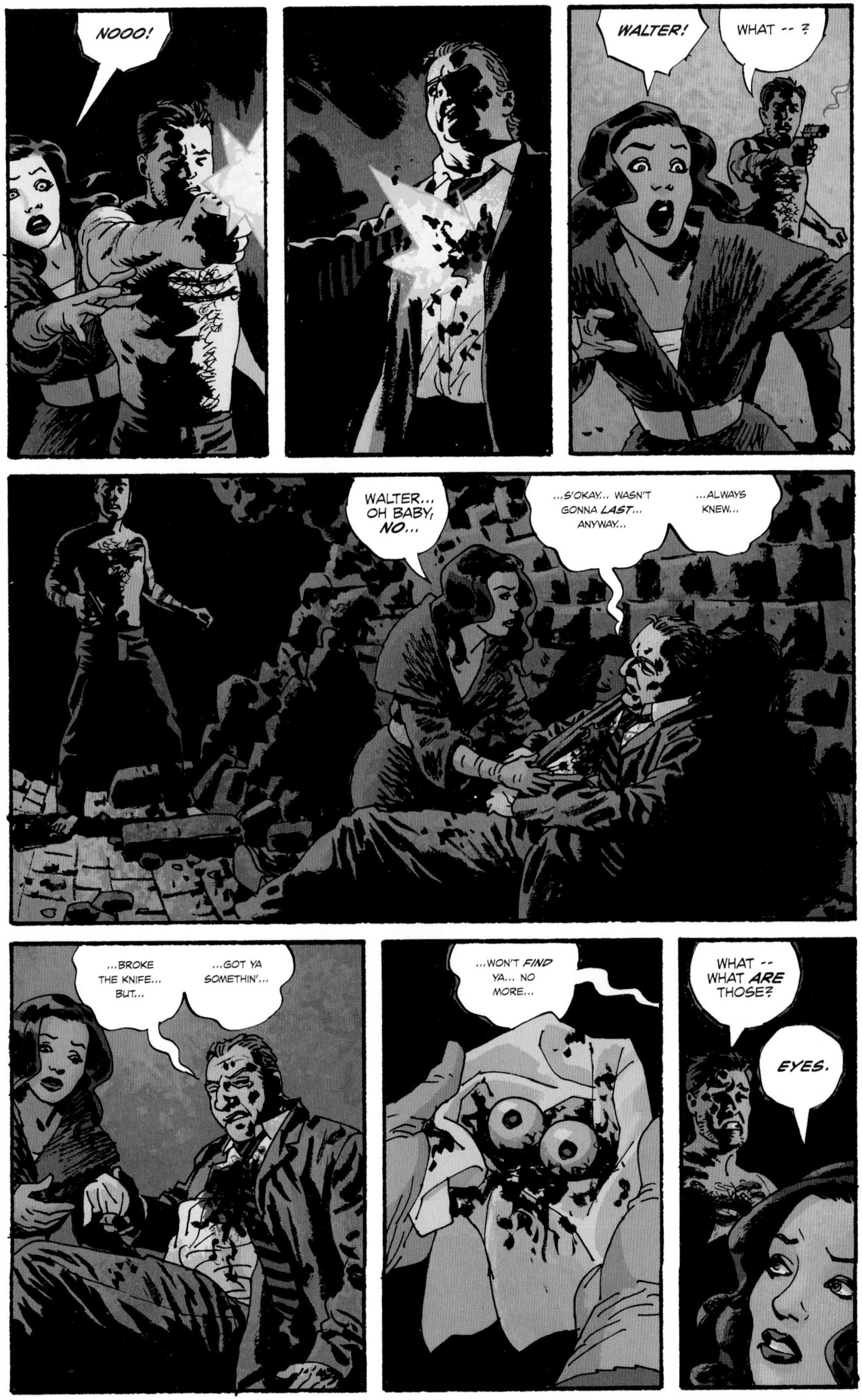
NOOO!
WALTER!
WHAT -- ?
WALTER... OH BABY, NO...
...S'OKAY... WASN'T GONNA LAST... ANYWAY...
...ALWAYS KNEW...
...BROKE THE KNIFE... BUT...
...GOT YA SOMETHIN'...
...WON'T FIND YA... NO MORE...
WHAT -- WHAT ARE THOSE?
EYES.

...HEY, 'MEMBER IN *PARIS*...?

...WHAT TH' OLD LADY SAID...

...ABOUT THE *RIBBON* 'ROUND THE WORLD...?

YES. I REMEMBER EVERYTHING...

I C'N *FEEL* IT... I...

...

WHAT...? JO, I DON'T UNDERSTAND...

I THOUGHT HE -- HE *BROUGHT* YOU TO *THEM*?

IT'S OKAY, HANK.

I DIDN'T UNDERSTAND EITHER...

C'MON... WE NEED TO GET OUT OF HERE...

IT'S DAYS BEFORE THE BODIES ARE FOUND, IN WHAT'S LEFT OF THE TUNNELS.

AND CROOKED COP WALTER BOOKER BECOMES A *HERO* IN DEATH...

HE AND HIS PARTNER, *VICTIMS* OF THE SAME CULT THEY WERE INVESTIGATING.

WHO ARE *ALSO* BLAMED FOR THE MURDER OF SYLVIA RAINES AND HER UNBORN CHILD.

San Fran...

OP DIES
SOLVING
MURDER

MORE LIES, HANK THINKS ...

...AND SHE'S THE *PRETTIEST LIE* OF THEM ALL.

WHAT ARE YOU THINKING?

JUST THAT I'M *FREE*...

BUT IT FEELS *WRONG* SOMEHOW. I DON'T KNOW WHY.

HANK STILL CAN'T HELP IT. HIS HEART BREAKS JUST LOOKING AT HER.

LOST IN DREAMS OF THEIR NEW LIFE, IN A NEW CITY SOMEWHERE...

...BUT HE WISHES HE COULD CRY FOR WHAT HE LOST.

IS IT GOING TO *WORK*?

YES, THE BISHOP *PREPARED* IT HIMSELF...

IT'S BEEN OVER A *WEEK* SINCE HE CUT IT OUT OF THE WOMAN.

DON'T QUESTION HIS WAYS.

HAVE *FAITH*, BROTHER.

AND SEE OUR MASTER *REBORN*.

WAAAHHHHH...

FROM A DISTANT SHORE, HE HEARS THEIR CALL.

A CHANT, A CURSE, AND A BLESSING, ALL AT ONCE.

IT'S HARDER THAN HE REMEMBERS, BEING BROUGHT INTO THE WORLD.

HE MOLDS THE BODY TO SUIT HIMSELF, WITH GREAT EFFORT.

GAAAHHH... FAAAHHH...

AND IT'S ONLY THEN THAT BISHOP *REALIZES* WHAT THE OLD COP MEANT...

...GNNN... AHHH...

THAT HE WASN'T *TRYING* TO KILL HIM.

THAT... THAT *BASTARD*...

HE *BLINDED* ME...

Epilogue

I started having trouble sleeping, after that day in the library.

I'd wake from dreams of strange men prodding and poking at my limbs...

Or of me and Jo walking along the beach... Her voice washed out by the crashing waves.

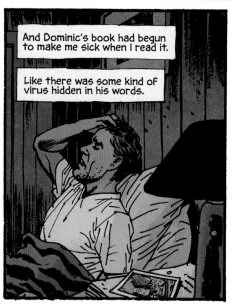

And Dominic's book had begun to make me sick when I read it.

Like there was some kind of virus hidden in his words.

Still, I had the picture...

Him and the woman who I *should* have thought was Jo's grandmother...

But that isn't what I thought.

No, what I thought was *impossible*.

WINGATE
Asylum

SIGN RIGHT THERE, SIR... AND I'LL NEED TO SEE YOUR I.D.

SOMEONE'LL BE HERE IN A *MINUTE* TO TAKE YOU BACK.

JUST HAVE A SEAT.

THANKS.

It had been at least three years since I'd seen my father.

And that last time, he'd tried to strangle me.

While raving about *saving me* from "them."

After that, his meds had been doubled.

HERE YOU GO, JUST *SHOUT* IF YOU NEED HELP.

So I wasn't expecting much...

DAD...?

HEY... IT'S NICK. *NICKY.*

DAD?

I KNOW YOU DON'T WANT TO SEE ME, BUT ... I NEED YOUR HELP.

SEE, I'VE BEEN STARING AT THIS PICTURE FOR MONTHS...

AND I THINK, MAYBE... I THINK *YOU* TOOK IT?

BACK IN THE 50S...?

I NEED TO KNOW WHO THIS WOMAN *IS*, DAD...

...WOMAN...?

It feels like I'm actually going to get an answer...

THAT... IT'S... IT'S...

But then the old man just starts *laughing*...

And not the right kind.

The kind that makes you want to burst your eardrums.

The kind you hear in your nightmares.

And I realize, that's all I've got.

END OF BOOK ONE

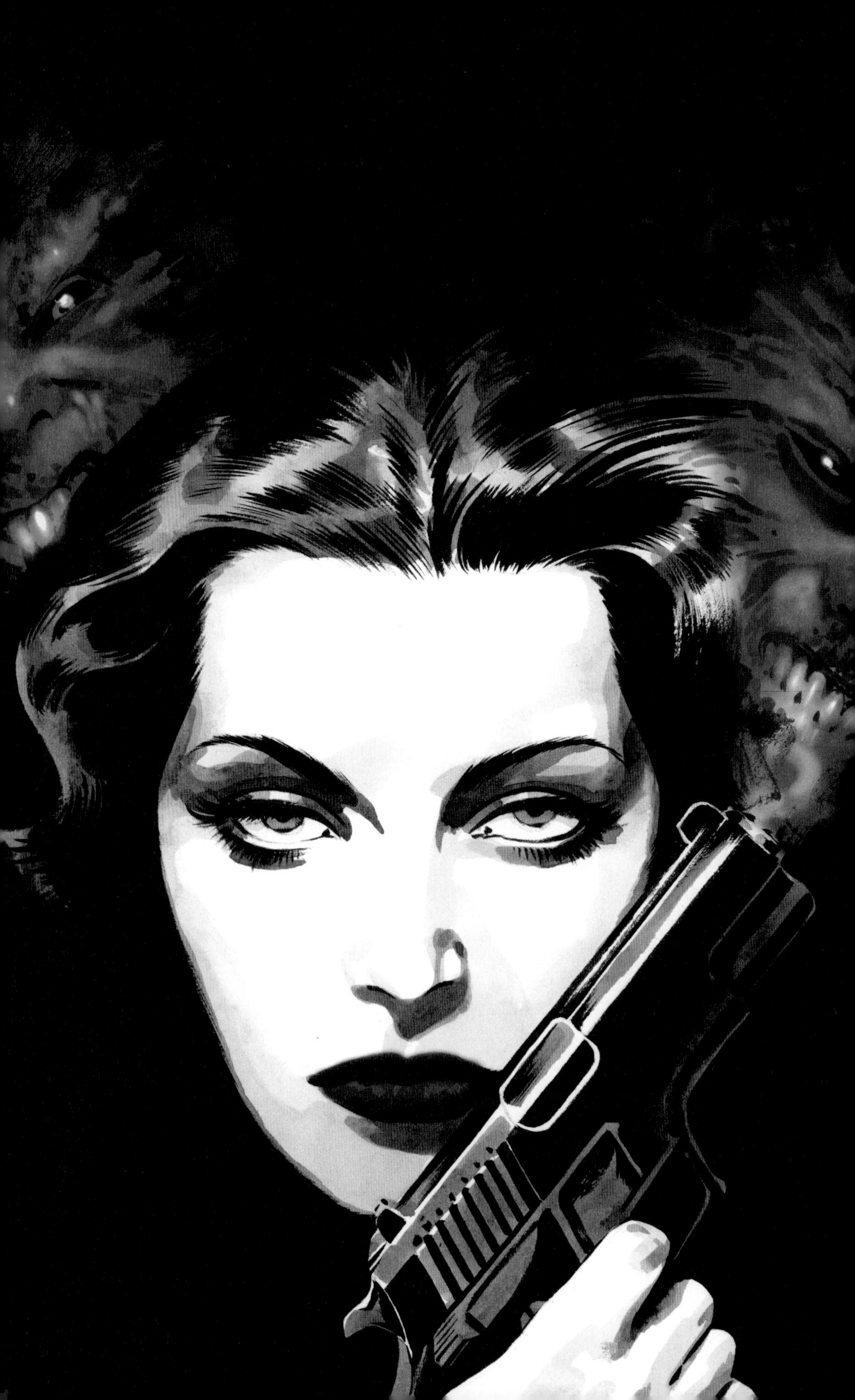

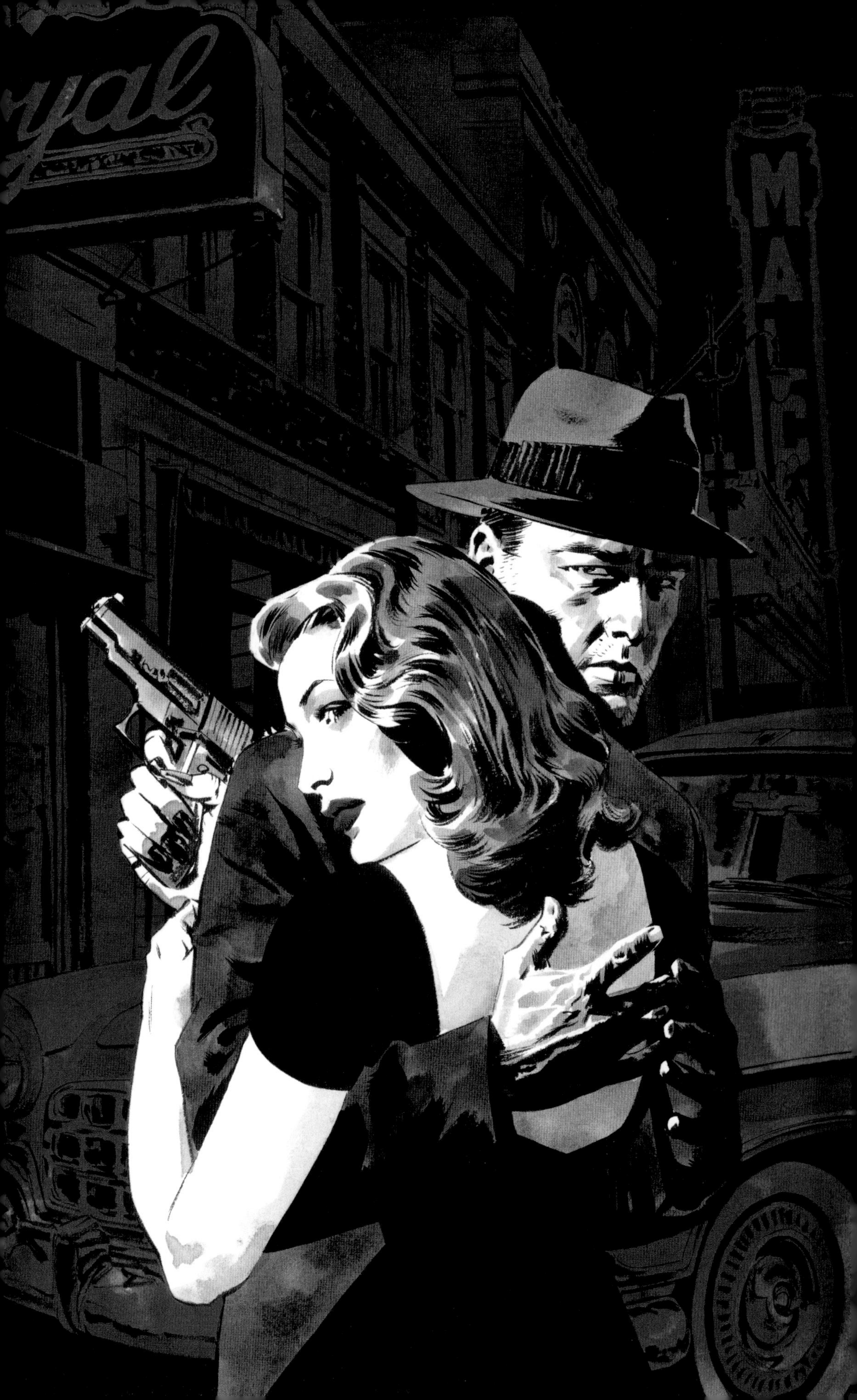

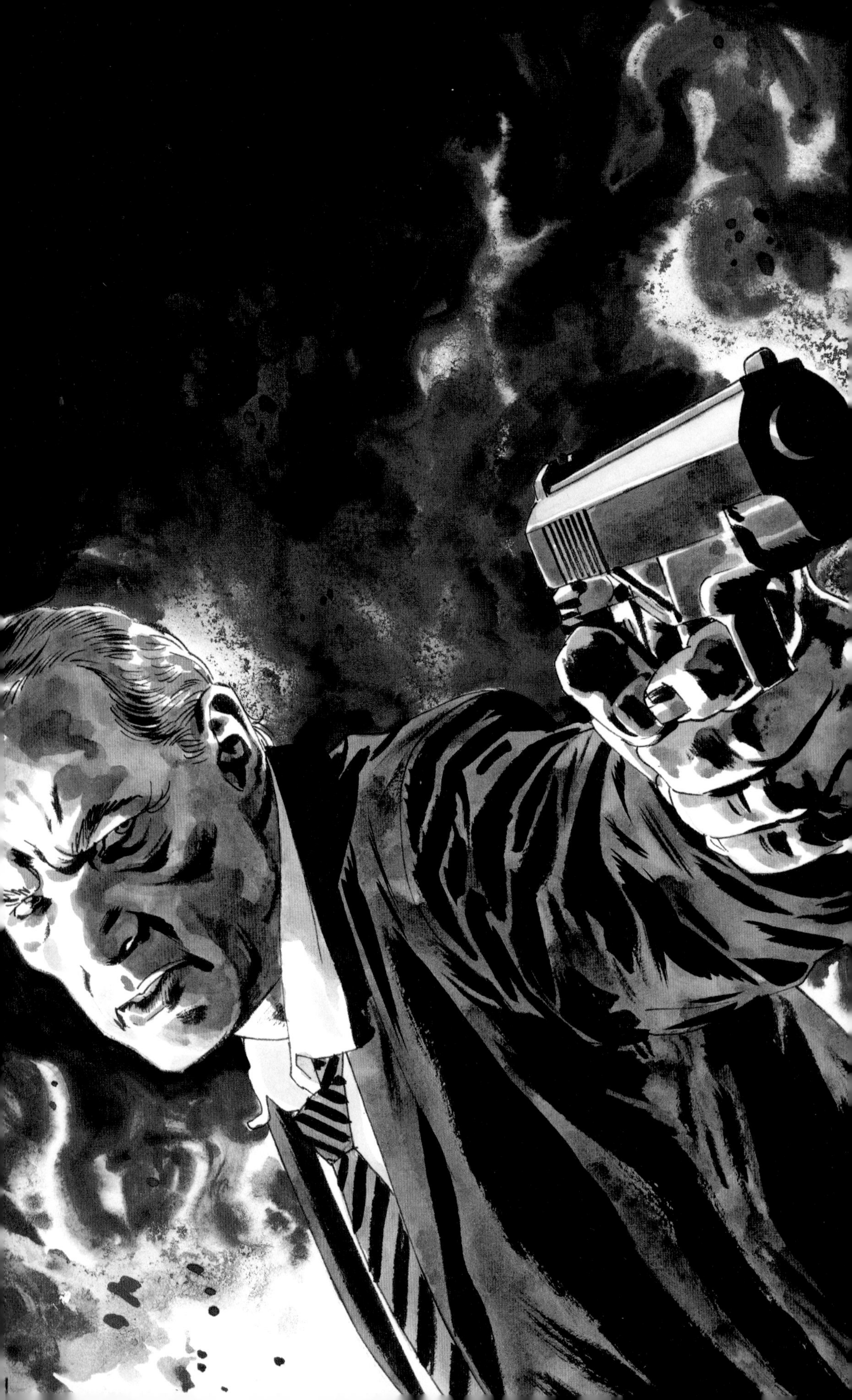

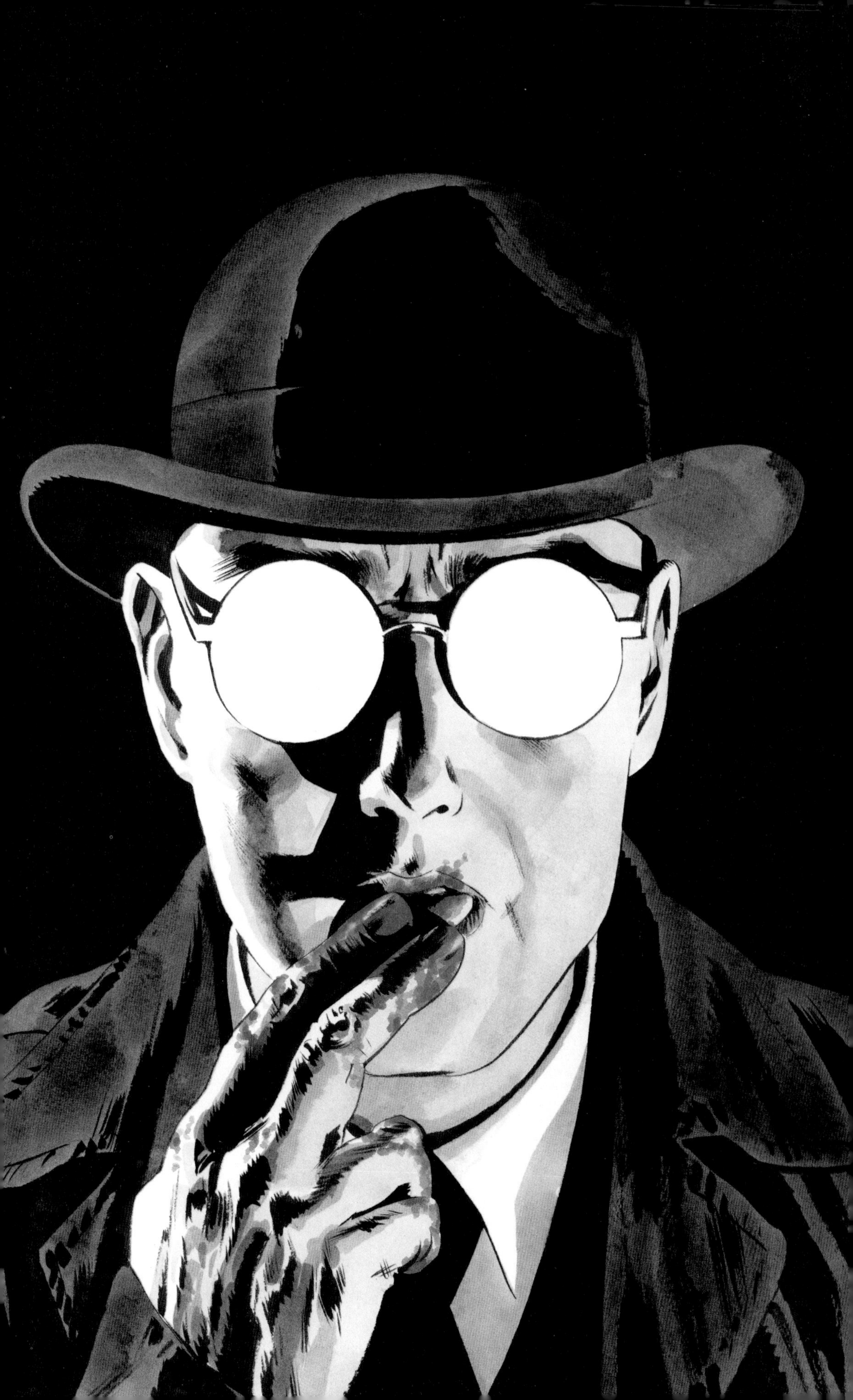

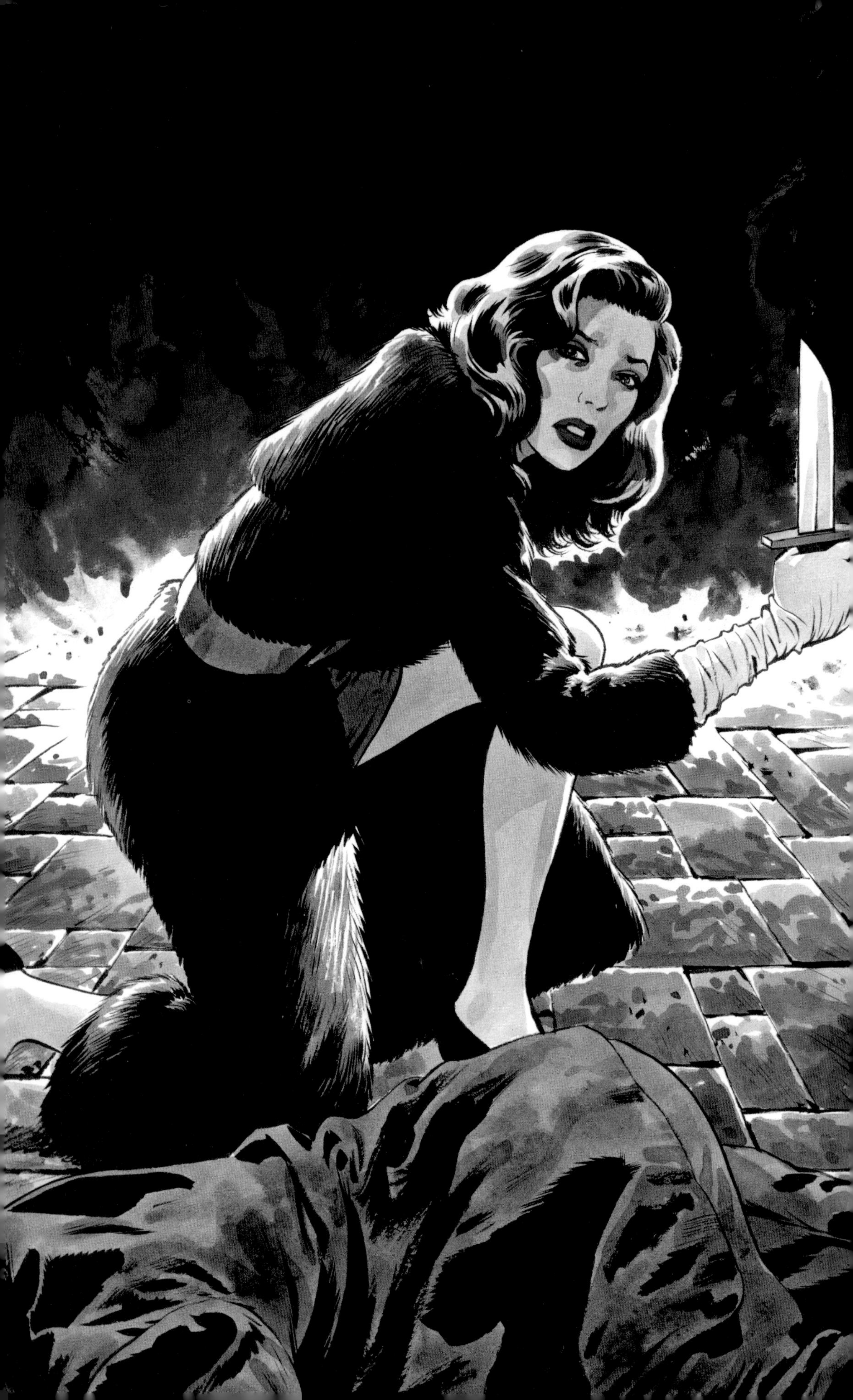

Discover the world of Brubaker and Phillips...

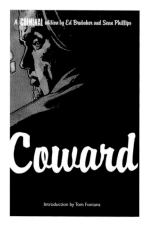